UNUSUAL ENCOUNTERS

Unusual Encounters: *Volume Two, Part One*

(paperback) ISBN: 9798424632624
(hardback) ISBN: 9781088016886

A publication of Tall Pine Books
|| *tallpinebooks.com*

*Printed in the United States of America

UNUSUAL ENCOUNTERS

VOLUME TWO: PART ONE

Azi Soki

CONTENTS

CHAPTER 1

SANCTUM

Shrine Pass, Redcliff Eagle County, Colorado
Elevation: 11,094 ft
Coordinates: 39 degrees 32' 50" N Latitude
106 degrees 14' 32" W Longitude

"HAVE YOU READ the Letters?" Elder Enoch asked him.

"I haven't opened them yet" Brother Dominick replied, shaking his head.

Both men were walking up the famous shrine pass, in between the pine woodlands, the wide path gave a beautiful scenic view, that seemed to extend farther than the eyes could see, stretching out miles into the horizon.

It's been a few days now, since Brother Dominick's plane crossed the Atlantic Ocean and landed in the United States, then later on that first day, he made his way into the tall corridors of the mount of the Holy Cross Cloister.

He was taken aback by the Gold Monastery's surrounding of nature, the vast array of forestry.

Its essence of nature also contributed greatly to it's slight air of mystery, so enigmatic in fact that one would think as if its own intentions are to hide and somehow camouflage itself within the wild landscape.

"You'll have to, eventually" Elder Enoch replied, a tall, dark-toned man, of very strong stature and authority, also known to many, previously as Brother Enoch, but very recently has now become an Elder ordained under the Order of the Priest Superior Clem Kedezih...whom Brother Dom has yet to meet. Elder Enoch had kindly volunteered to be Brother Dom's guide and mentor, helping him transition properly into the Gold monastery's structure and life.

Both men wearing the standard robes based on responsibility and ranking, Brother Dom had on a brown robe with a gold sash around the waist.

Elder Enoch was wearing a red-orange robe with a gold sash around the waist, the gold fabric was also embroidered at the cuffs of both men's robes emphasizing the monastery's gold-toned mascot colors.

They had walked a short distance into the pine woodlands and now turned back around, heading back toward the monastery walking under the vast, open, and clear blue sky. The entire scenery from the sky to grassland was nothing short of spectacular. There was a very brief conversation, as both men took great pleasure in absorbing the bliss of nature all around them, the birds, the butterflies, and more.

"Uh...Elder Enoch? What are you doing?"

Brother Dom asked as they were walking, Elder Enoch had suddenly stopped in his tracks and stooped down, then touched the ground, by placing his right palm flat on the dirt, gently as one would place a hand on a baby's chest, caring to feel their heartbeat. He then rose back up quickly dusting off his hands he said "there's three men on horseback, coming in our direction, from behind us, exactly two kilometers away, but approaching very quickly, two on cream gold-colored Andalusian horses, one in the middle, on a dark brown Friesian horse..."

"Whoa, hold on a second...Elder Enoch... and you know this how?" as Brother Dom asked the question, suddenly the sounds of galloping horses echoed in the distance.

Brother Dominick couldn't believe his eyes, "wait here..." Elder Enoch says as he walks toward the three men on horses. They were hooded figures, you could barely see their faces...the one in the middle...the one sitting on a dark brown Friesian horse was the leader, without a doubt.

All three men, powerful in stature were very intimidating to look at... the two on either side of the leader, wore each, very distinguished colored hooded coats...the horse rider on the left of the leader, was fully clothed in gold-tone garment with a gold-toned staff of about five feet long, being held by him sideways, his hooded tunic had specific intricate gold markings on them; what caught Brother Dominick's attention on this horse rider was this peculiar golden glow...how is that possible? He thought.

He turned over to look at the horse rider on the right

side of the leader, he was clothed in silver, metallic-toned garment. He seemed to be a higher-ranking par excellence warrior, some type of a first graded knight, with a silver-toned sword hanging sideways in its scabbard, the horse riders were very commanding in stature...but the one in the middle was the dominant of all three.

There was something quite odd about the three individuals, they didn't look ordinary. Instead, they looked... beatific. "But how could that be?" he thought. Elder Enoch was speaking with them...but there were no gestures of dialogue, from where Brother Dom could see, their mouths were not moving, even Elder Enoch, with his hands behind his back, standing looking up at the three men on horses, he was looking specifically at the one in the middle...the leader.

Brother Dom's rational mind couldn't accept it, but he was witnessing the undeniable realization that...all four men were communicating through a far superior exchange, through...thoughts? "No way?" He whispered.

Suddenly, the leader lifted both hands and pulled his hood down as he looked straight at Brother Dominick, from a distance of about ten feet apart.

"What in the world?" Brother Dom whispered as he locked eyes with the man on the Friesian horse, his dark eyes like burning coal were looking, staring at Brother Dom, he felt it deep into his very soul; he had a knowing, fatherly, authoritative look on Brother Dom.

He was held frozen by the mysterious horse rider when suddenly he feels a strong, abnormal wind wave, so powerful in fact, that his hair and robe moved along with his entire body, the wind was blowing one hundred thirty-three degrees south-east bound, physically moving, transporting Brother Dominick towards the four men's direction.

The wind was coming from behind him and moving in forwarding motion ahead where the horse riders stood. Losing control, his feet dragging, sliding against the grass and dirt. Brother Dominick had to stretch both arms out in front of him, in an attempt to catch himself from falling forward, grasping desperately anything in his path for balance.

His gaze was on the ground. He lifted his head and halted, startled by the leader, he was staring at him, he then smiled genuinely at Brother Dominick in a way, a father would smile proudly at his son, Brother Dom felt strange...a knowing of this man on the Friesian horse, he had extremely dark hair, greys showing at the beard, and on either side of his temples, right above the ears.

Brother Dom was getting so caught up and captivated by him, that he didn't realize, the distance between him and the four men became short, he has been walking toward the group of men ...which by now Brother Dom was certain, this so-called wind was not normal wind... but instead had a mind of its own, pulling Brother Dom closer to the one man on the Friesian horse, the leader.

"Enough" Brother Dom whispered slowly, breathing hard as he closed his eyes, rubbing them with his fingers "this is not real" he whispered again to himself, reopened his eyes... and he suddenly notices that the three horseback riders were gone...vanished out of thin air, in the space of three short seconds.

He then sees Elder Enoch walking alone back toward him, hands folded behind his back.

"Dominick"

"Was that all real or just my imagination...but I saw it with my own eyes?"

Brother Dominick was so shocked because he couldn't deny it, he knew what he saw and as proof of that, there were traces, tracks on the grass, of his footsteps fighting against the strange wind, propelling him forward, ... his feet sliding on the ground.

The entire footpath and steps were a toral distance of five feet traced on the ground. Elder Enoch heard quietly as Brother Dominick described what he already knew as he was present.

Brother Dom then went quiet suddenly as a strong realization hit him. While they were entering the monastery, both men were about to take opposite paths in the outside corridors of the gold monastery. Brother Dom realized that he had just spent an entire thirty minutes talking about a strange, mysterious event in which Elder Enoch himself was very much apart. "Who is Elder Enoch?" Brother Dominick thought, but his heart, skipped a beat when suddenly the very second, he asked that question internally, something strange happened.

Both men were walking in opposite directions as they parted ways in the outdoor hallway. Brother Dom had stood watching Elder Enoch retreating back, a distant robed silhouette.

Suddenly Elder Enoch stopped in his tracks, he slowly turns around, now standing, he looks at him, Brother Dom was startled and a bit intimidated, he raised his right hand towards his chest, his heart was beating fast, as he realized so far, the events, he had witnessed defied every rational law of nature, and now this...

"He heard my thoughts" Brother Dominick whispered

Elder Enoch stared at him, smiling kindly from fifteen feet away, "How did he do that?"

"Be opened..."

"Who said that?" Brother Dominick spoke out loud looking around him, no one was there. Except...there stood Elder Enoch staring at him, a very solemn expression on his face.

"Be opened, Dom"

Brother Dominick saw that Elder Enoch's mouth was not moving. "But how is he doing that, speaking into my mind".

"Be opened" Brother Dom heard it for the third time, it was Elder Enoch's voice answering his thoughts. Then Elder Enoch turned back around with a brief smile and continued walking the rest of the way in the opposite direction.

"What is this place?" Brother Dominick said.

He had a plan, tomorrow, he will return to the shrine pass, into the pine woodlands, and explore the area, he might find some clues, as he decided to investigate.

After a series of solid investigations on these peculiar occurrences, Brother Dominick's next step will be, to find the highest authority in the monastic hierarchy and clergy... The Priest Superior Clem Kedezih, and report to him all the strange accounts at the gold monastery, including some of the key members of the clergy such as the mysterious Elder Enoch or better yet he could contact his cousin, the commissioner.

CHAPTER 2

THE MAZE OF KADESH-BARNEA

EIGHTEEN HOURS LATER, four-thirty am the next day, Brother Dominick wakes up, alert on a mission, to go and explore the pine woodlands, by the time he walks outside, the sun would be rising, which means he will also be able to 'catch dawn'. He had looked at the weather forecast the night prior, all clear sky, sunny high seventies. Brother Dom got ready, stepped out of his room, and walked quietly down the long corridor, even though his room was located on the west side of the giant cathedral. He could hear the large bell chime four o'clock in the morning for the brothers and Elders scheduled to serve on the morning session of worship and the practice of waiting in silence.

He took a map with him, Brother Dom finally made it out of the interior establishment without being noticed.

Now step two, the large, tall metal gates covered with beautiful green foliage hanging that encircled the entire perimeter of the 2.64 Acres compound. He was at an absolute standstill, not knowing where to go, he almost gave up on the mission, until he saw his way out...as his eyes were looking around, they stopped on a path, about eleven feet from where he stood, Brother Dom thought, "no, not a path, it's a maze" it was, in fact, the famous maze of Kadesh-Barnea.

He read many stories in the ancient archive called "The map of happenings" and came upon the chapter titled maze of Kadesh-Barnea, which was about hard to believe stories, there was one, in particular, that was difficult to grasp; that of a man, whom according to legends was a friar named Bernard Gerard, he lived or rather spent most of this time walking inside the maze of Kadesh-Barnea, one day the friar ventured further into the maze until he inadvertently reached what is now known today as the Glory Dome, he suddenly sees a man, a very mysterious man, wearing a robe with a hood on, of purple and red color, and the man asked the Friar to come closer, as they were standing about twelve feet apart, the friar was a bit afraid as the man in the purple and red robe was very powerful, imposing and possessed such a peaceful but yet intimidating countenance.

As the Friar got closer, he noticed the mysterious man had both hands folded behind his back. He came close about three feet out, suddenly the man stretches both hands out right in front of him...the friar got close enough and hesitantly touched both hands. Suddenly he could barely stand, he felt heavy, out of breath, and although he couldn't see clearly, he noticed with his blurred vision that the man's eyes were on him, seeming as if he's known him all his life, then he looked down at his hands, which prompted the friar to look at the man's hands and he saw writings on the man's hands, the left hand had the markings "Eph" but he couldn't see the right hand, because the man had a very strange propensity to luminesce.

It then became so bright inside the Glory Dome that the abnormally glowing light enveloped the entire chapel and the friar blacked out... hours later, he was found by the other Brothers on the floor of the Glory Dome, laying eyes closed, well and breathing...but something very strange was happening to the friar. Bright light, pure bright light was pulsing through the pores on his forearms...

"This is absolutely incoherent," Brother Dominick said as he remembered that strange account he read from the book on his dresser.

Brother Dominick was awestruck by the beauty inside the maze of Kadesh-Barnea, the big maze stretched miles long, out in the four cardinal directions: an entrance North, South, East, West, leading into different areas of the gold monastery.

He had to make a choice, which way to go, so Brother Dominick took one path at random, ready to set himself on a longer than usual journey, he walked slowly and chose North, then stops, startled to see a man standing on the West sided path of the Maze, Brother Dominick became curious and turned, walking toward the stranger.

He noticed the man was tending to some flower shrubs and plants that seemed to expand further, toward what Brother Dom came to realize was a garden, He was holding an herb snip, on one hand, his gaze lowered and he saw a pruner on the ground by the man's feet.

"Well, that's odd, why do gardening at four in the morning?" He thought as he approached the man, now fully engaged unto the western side of the maze.

Brother Dom took a closer look at the man's robe and did a double-take, he couldn't believe his eyes, the purple and gold colors on this man's robes immediately gave away the identity of this mysterious gardener... "Monsignor..." Bro Dom whispered

"You should take this path and continue all the way; it will get you there faster"

The stranger said, who was none other than the Priest Superior Clem Kedezih, Brother Dominick realized in awe, the Priest Superior was the only entity in the entire monasterial hierarchy, in both premises of the silver and gold cloister, the only one who wears both combination of purple and gold with the precise symmetrical patterns of the biblical cross in silver carved on the yoke of his robe, which covers the Priest's shoulders. "Dominick" The Priest Superior called Brother Dom, who was startled out of his thoughts...the Priest was smiling, for some unknown reason.

Brother Dominick suddenly was certain that the Priest Superior knew all about his life, to the very close details, his personal quest, his innermost ambition; and his life even prior to him joining the brotherhood.

At the same time, Brother Dom could see the vivid, joyful expression in the Priest Superior's coffee burnt brown eyes.

He had this inner knowing that the monsignor possessed some type of unknown power and authority far greater than a priest or even a human for that matter. He frowned slightly as the Priest Superior, smiled brighter at Brother Dom knowingly, but he felt very much at ease with the Priest and at peace, the kind of peace that was very foreign to him. It was startling, he didn't what to do.

He backed away, walking backward, further into the western side of the maze as shown by the Priest Superior. The latter had stopped his gardening activity at this point. He stood briefly with both hands folded in front of him, watching Brother Dom, disturbingly attentive, he then returned to tending the flowers.

Brother Dominick now turned forward walking two-three steps deeper into the western side, suddenly he feels a tangible soft breeze, behind him, strong enough with a whoosh sound, to the point where his shoulder-length hair moved.

Startled, he stops in his tracks and turned around only to see ten feet away from where he stood. The Priest Superior was...gone...as if he was never there, except for the evidence of the well-tended red roses and white hydrangeas.

"How in the world did he do that?" Brother Dom said out loud.

"Maybe he...no there's no way, impossible" Brother Dom shook his head, dismissing the mere idea that the Priest Superior could have possibly made himself disappear.

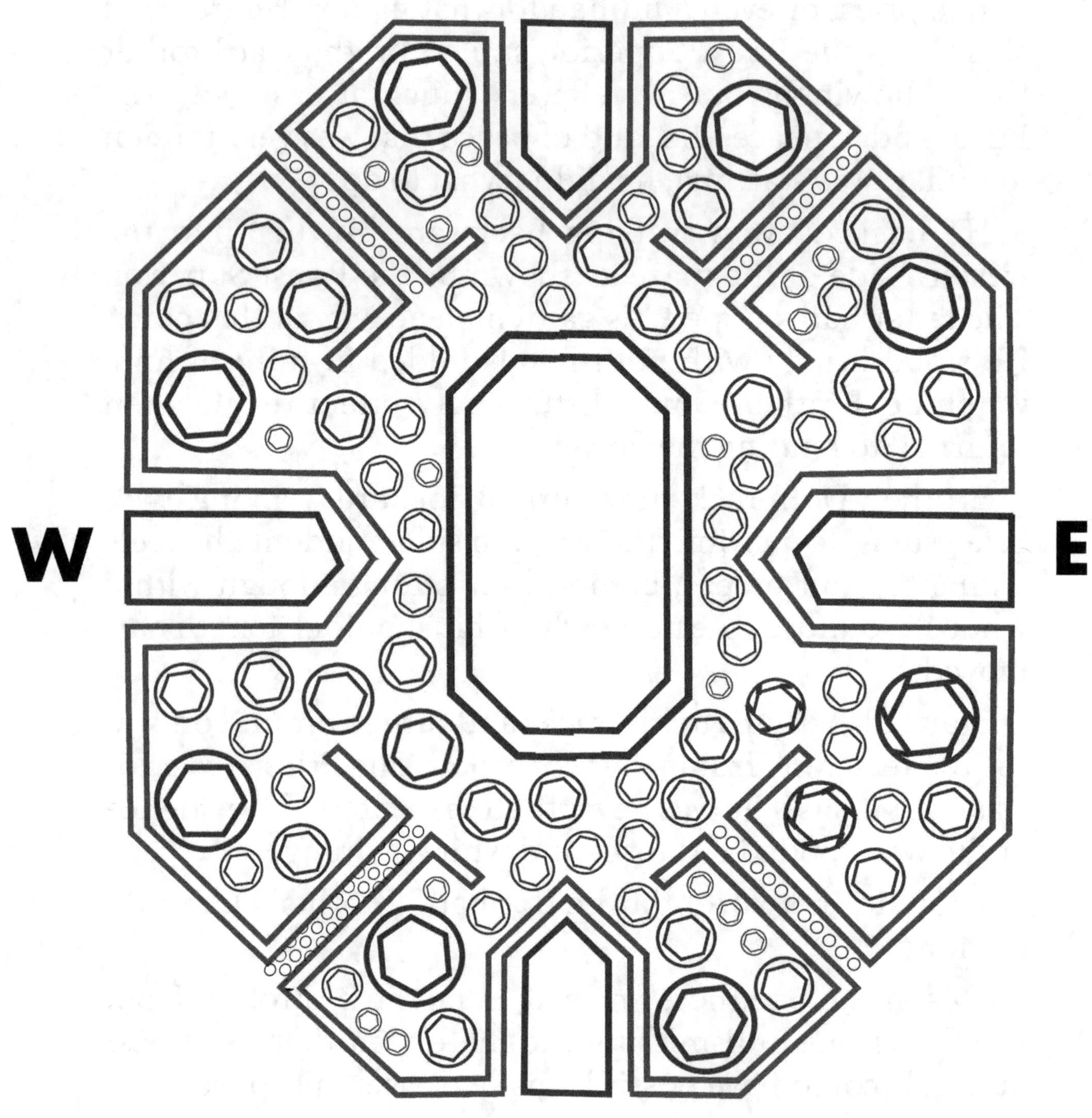
N
W
E
S

MAZE OF KADESH-BARNEA

Brother Dominick continued on to the western path of the big maze, as he was making his way to leave the maze, he couldn't help but feel that the Priest Superior Clem Kedezih is not who the Brotherhood thinks he is...standing there gardening, looking all ordinary, how did he know where Brother Dom was headed? He never told anyone of his plans. He was much more powerful than he cared to reveal, Brother Dom was certain of it, but he wasn't willing to dig deeper into the Priest's identity.

"Oh, there it is, finally...one eternity later" Brother Dominick whispered facetiously. As he stepped out of the maze and right into the middle of the most amazing sight of nature he's ever seen, the pine woodlands...which he has been one side of it with Elder Enoch, but has never been to this area of the woodlands before, far out into the horizon in an open sky, he could see the sun rising, there was beautiful warm weather expected today. "Ok let's get to work" Brother Dom then pulled out a map of the monastery, and took a closer look at the courtyard right outside the Maze of Kadesh-Barnea, "that's where I am right now, so I guess continue Northwest" he said, as he followed the direction from the map, he noticed that the sky, although sunny gave an impression as if rain was coming, which was very odd, he thought...

Brother Dominick realized he has been walking for fifteen minutes exploring the breathtaking pine woodlands, when suddenly a rumble, very loud rumble sounded from the sky, lightning, and peals of thunder grew louder as it descended into the ground crashing, between the tall grass, about five feet in behind him. "What? Lightning but no rain?..." another lightning wave suddenly cracked into the sky down along with a clapping sound of thunder.

At this point, Brother Dominick realized that this was not a normal occurrence as it was an absolute contradiction to the beautiful scenery of the bright sun rising, and dry ground, no clouds in the sky suggesting rain...only lightning waves followed by peals of thunder. Brother Dominick was amazed. So, he took off running forward as the lightning waves were not hitting at random, there were mostly coming from behind him in forward progression. He knew, finding shelter was the safest option. So, he goes further into the beautiful shrine pass.

Suddenly Brother Dom stops in his tracks, it was now full daylight, sun shining bright with sun rays piercing through the tall pine trees, creating various 'holes' of light. "A cabin...thank God" Brother Dominick whispered as he walked toward it, the lightning and peals of thunder were still occurring. Although this weather was new to him, Brother Dominick was all too familiar with the scenery... born of the Ute Mountain Ute Tribe, here in Colorado, Brother Dom was used to nature and the wild, since childhood. He never realized after leaving his home for the Aegean Sea, that ironic enough, he would get transferred back to his native town once again.

Boom! Thunderclaps sounded again, with loud rumbles, all the while the birds were chirping, sky clear with sunshine.

Brother Dom saw the lightning waves behind the tall

trees. He ran all the to the cabin's door, he tried the door and it opened effortlessly.

Brother Dom didn't have the time to think whose cabin it was, as now he heard a series of thunderclaps sounding, cracking into the sky with loud rumbles again, louder than the previous ones.

He immediately went inside the cabin, hurriedly closed the door shut behind him, the wooden cabin was larger inside, more space than he thought, and it was made out of solid enough wood to withstand any weather condition, he hoped so at least.

Suddenly Brother Dominick hears a rustling further into the cabin, there was enough daylight, coming from the open window...for him to see that there was a man, he was tall, with imposing stature...due to the contrast of light and shadows, some part of the room was not quite visible, as a result, Brother Dominick couldn't see his face clearly, he was seated on a massive armchair, each arm on an armrest.

He was wearing a robe and had white hair shoulder length, and a white beard, Brother Dominick was still standing by the door, now intimidated to move further; the much older man had a very odd...regality about him, power almost frightening but riveting at the same time, the man must be one of the monastery's elder or so he thought. Brother Dominick tried to see much clear by squinting his eyes, but still, he couldn't see the facial features of the elderly man.

He looked to his right, which would be the left side of the older man, there was a chest with a globe set on it.

Brother Dom saw something physically impossible happening to the globe, it was turning of its own volition, and as it turned, golden writing started to appear, in different areas and continents of the globe.

A sizzling sound suddenly broke the silence, the elderly man was staring, observing Brother Dom, he could feel it and didn't know how there was such undeniable potency, the man looked like someone who was aware of himself and what he was capable of, to a high extent.

"Ok…this is weird, let me get out of here" as he barely finished his sentence, suddenly Brother Dominick couldn't stay standing, he involuntary fell on his knees right in front of the door facing the mysterious older man, who was still sited about twelve feet from him, and haven't moved a finger. Brother Dom could barely breathe, his body giving out.

"Who are you--, humph!"

It happened…Brother Dominick witnessed the most surreal, unexplainable event he has ever seen in his entire existence.

A pair of single electromagnetic waves of white and golden lightning bolts shot out of the elderly man's hands.

Brother Dominick saw that the lightning bolts emerged from the powerful man's index finger and thumbs. Both the left and right arms, were still rested on the armchairs, and the fingers were splayed out, there was enough sunlight for him to see that actual lightning bolts were coming from the index and thumb specifically.

Suddenly as lightning bolts came out from the elder

man's hands, then it started making its way in zigzag motion on the wooden floor but straightforward headed for Brother Dom, in two specific paths, in the blink of an eye, he felt high voltage going into his body, and he couldn't stop shaking, violently.

Then something much more extraordinary took place, while his knees were now glued to the floor, after the lightning waves dissipated into him, consumed in his body. one single thick electron wave of pure gold, liquid like substance suddenly comes out of...the man's mouth...

Brother Dominick was petrified, realizing this was no ordinary man he was dealing with. Brother Dom could see clear enough even through the shadows covering the older man's face, that the latter had just opened his mouth, in an o shape and gold liquid came out of the man's mouth, traveling downward onto the wooden floor, all twelve feet straight forward, making its way up to Brother Dominick's torso and as soon as the gold lightning wave reached his throat...He was confused and very much afraid for his life because he lost control of his body, his physical body had an intellect of its own, not following at all what his mind was resisting, his mouth involuntarily opened... his eyes widened as he was witnessing himself, ingurgitating the gold lightning wave.

And the room went completely dark...

CHAPTER 3

AFTERMATH

BROTHER DOMINICK REALIZED it wasn't the room that went dark, but instead, he had briefly closed his eyes, for seconds, then opened them, only to find himself...in his bedroom, on his bed ...with two men standing over him, staring, he recognized the first one to be Elder Enoch, but didn't recognize the other man "Dominick, Brother Dominick"

Brother Dom tried to recollect and clear out his mind, then remembered suddenly the entire series of events from this morning.

"The man on the chair" he whispered

"Brother Dominick, are you able to speak? We can't hear you" Elder Enoch asked.

"Hmm...I think he temporarily lost his voice," the second older man said.

"Are you positive?" Elder Enoch asked then added

"Brother Dominick, this is father Andrew of the west wing, he is also a physician, you've been out for five hours" Brother Dom was watching them, listening.

"Father Andrew ran exams while you were out" Elder Enoch saw the question in Brother Dom's eyes, and he could hear his thoughts.

"What happened?" Brother Dom was trying to say.

"One of the brothers found you laying on the ground by the west entrance of the maze, at the great fountain, near the garden, he was returning from his morning prayer and decided to take a detour through the maze,

"you're fine" he added quickly, as he read the worried expression on Brother Dominick's face.

He looked at the brother intensely with an odd expression.

"Father Andrew, would that be all? Are we all set?"

"Yes, judging from the exam, he will be recovering his voice within the next twenty-four to seventy-two hours...in the meantime, I suggest he rests"

Elder Enoch nodded briefly, thanking him, and waited silently until the father left the room.

Brother Dom sat on his bed, his back against the headboard, "Dominick, listen to me very carefully"

"Sure, it seems, that's all I'm able to do at this point," he thought, giving him a pointed look.

Elder Enoch chuckled, amused as he understood.

Then the Elder's expression changed and became very attentive and serious. He looked at Brother Dominick with such fatherly affection and said "there's a message for you in those letters…the Letter of Rise and the Letter of Demand, you must open them"

"Dominick, honestly, I believe that you being so stubborn and deliberately refusing to open these letters, then being the extreme skeptic that you are; about your transition into the Gold Brotherhood…all this triggered the predicament you're in right now. You can't escape this son."

Brother Dominick grabbed a notepad and pen then wrote "Open them…"

"Hmm…I don't think that's a good idea" Elder Enoch said, leaning back on his chair.

"Please…" Brother Dom wrote on the notepad then held it up before him.

"Ok, I'll open it for you Dominick, but listen to me, you might be surprised by…you know let me just go ahead and _" Elder Enoch didn't finish his sentence and just opened the letter titled Letter of Rise, and read out loud.

To Pazz Lazar Takoda

Letter Of Rise -Eph-

"…And the Ancient of Days took his seat his vesture was like white snow,
and the hair of his head like pure wool…"
"Then comes the roaring of the thunder_ the
tremendous voice of his majesty"

"It rolls across the heavens and his lightning flashes in every direction.
For you are a holy people to the Lord your God, the Lord your God has chosen you to be a people for his own possession..."
"And you shall be to me a kingdom of Priests..."

As Elder Enoch read the Letter of Rise, Brother Dominick was in shock, the Elder called out his full legal name, from his native tribe, the Ute Mountain Ute Tribe. Right upon entering into the monastery years ago, Brother Dominick chose not to disclose his real name to the entire brotherhood, as he identifies more with Brother Dom, he also noticed two specific words being used often as Elder Enoch read the letter,

"Thunder and flashes of lightning" is just enough to remind him of the unforgettable phenomenon he experienced in the pine woodlands. The doctor who had left the room earlier, came back "Elder Enoch, you're needed at the Glory Dome" he said with the door slightly opened "I'll be heading over there in just a few minutes, thank you Doc"

As Doc closed the door, Elder Enoch turned back, facing

Brother Dominick, the latter had his gaze on the letter just read by him. The Letter of Rise, a mystical letter that he himself couldn't decipher the hidden message and he was sure there were multiple meanings behind it addressed to him personally.

"Thank you for your help with the letter, Elder Enoch means a lot."

Elder Enoch read Brother Dominick's note, as he raised it for him to see.

"Anytime son, you should get some rest, Doctor's orders."

then as he walked to the door, hand on the doorknob, he added "and free advice Dominick, true rest also does include the mind being at rest, putting aside thoughts and concerns...rest my friend" Brother Dominick nodded after the elder left, he decided to focus on rest and getting his speech back.

CHAPTER 4

AN ORDINARY DAY

Two days later...

Brother Dom was already up at 5 am, his speech was back as if nothing happened, no residual anomaly, Father Andrew, the Doctor had run some tests the day prior, late at night. He was amazed at how this mysterious temporary impediment came about and dissipated so quickly. Doc Andrew called it a supernatural occurrence far above science. Now 6:30 in the morning Brother Dominick got out of bed and was slowly pacing in his room, deep in thought. He then decides to go back to sleep for an extra hour, a few minutes later, as Brother Dom sat on his bed.

Suddenly he hears a rustling noise by the chest of drawers to his right. which were about two steps away from the bed, it was the third one down specifically where the rustling sound was coming from "maybe a squirrel or something"

Brother Dom quickly did a mental countdown 3...2...1,

he pulled the drawer, then pauses as he sees a book fall out right at his feet. He began to pick it up when something else inside the drawer catches his attention. He grabs the first item

"A spiritual maxim from Friar Gerard Bernard? Strange what's it doing here?"

The spiritual maxim parchment had the Glory Dome insignia on it 'GD', meaning separate from all the other libraries inside the monastery.

The Glory Dome had its own set of literature not opened to the public, that only the brotherhood was allowed to use and read strictly within the walls of the Glory Dome, never to be taken outside.

"Impossible" he whispered, although it was only one page from the parchment, the GD library kept such close catalog and coding of its books, that even one missing page found in his hand could result in him being temporarily sanctioned for stealing, when he never did such thing.

He looked closely at the brown piece of parchment paper then read the words Eph, which seemed to be a fragment of a word or maybe an abbreviation, "Wait I've seen this before" the three letters looked very familiar, then he remembered the Letter of Rise, form the pair of letters that mysteriously appeared in his folder on the airplane.

"Eph? what could this possibly mean" Brother Dom set the parchment down on the bed.

He was about to get up from the floor when he suddenly hears another rustling from the same third drawer. He kneels back down opens the drawer, then he sees a brown set of high-quality leather gloves with a parchment...

"No, not a parchment," he thought out loud, he then opened the folded paper, a letter, wait that's my letter 'Letter of Demand' from the airplane...but how?"

After he got ready for the day, as sleep was no longer in question, he decided to read the Letter of Demand. Brother Dominick saw that the back of the letter had his full birth name written on it and said 'for your eyes only'

Brother Dominick paused for a moment, before opening the Letter of Demand, He had a strange feeling that opening and reading this letter will somehow change his life from that moment on as if it hasn't already, Brother Dominick opened the letter then read, noticed something odd, the contents of the letter consisted of just one sentence written in the center of the paper, in perfect symmetry with the margins. Brother Dominick decided to read the contents of the letter out loud.

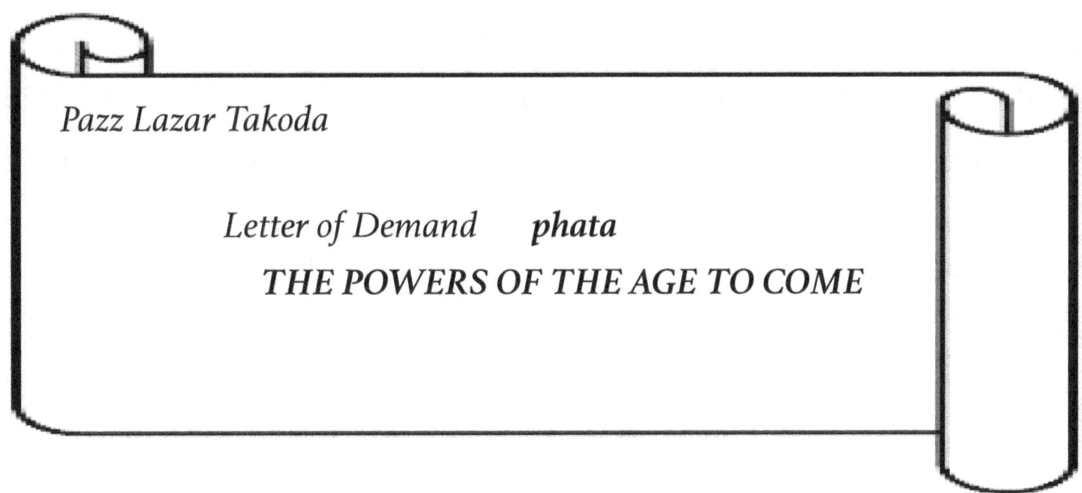

Pazz Lazar Takoda

Letter of Demand ***phata***

THE POWERS OF THE AGE TO COME

He suddenly felt tingling s ensations coming from the center of his chest all the way down to both hands, it went from tingling to a burning sensation, when...It happened.

Brother Dom was carefully observing his hands when visible electric waves, shot out of both his hands, which were close to each other.

Brother Dom's eyes widened in absolute awe and fear, He was completely undone and confused, breathing heavily, he held out his hands in front of him, trembling, and looking at them like they were foreign objects from a different galaxy, and not his own hands. "Dominick, what's wrong?" Elder Enoch said as he entered the room, Brother Dom was so out of composure he fell backward unto the wooden floor knocking some items on the night table along the way, shaking uncontrollably as his eyes were still glued to his hands, which were now merged in their electromagnetic waves' emissions, as he held out both his hands in front of him. Elder Enoch suddenly stopped in his tracks, he looked over Brother Dominick in the Direction of the window, someone else was in the room with them and Elder Enoch had that same expression of silent communication from back at the mountain, his expression resolute, he nodded briefly to the other person, stepped back and left the room.

Brother Dominick's mind was overwhelmed, he looked to this right and was startled, a man was standing there by the window, wearing the ancient garments of a knight with strong features. He looked familiar...then he remembered the legends of the Rogue Knights templar "wait that's not them" he felt his heartbeat accelerate, the visitor was not one of the Rogue knights, he was the one man on the Friesian horse in the pine woodlands, in fact, it was the one in the middle...who was staring at him that fateful day... It's him. The visitor smiled at him "who...what are you?"

Brother Dominick asked as his hands were still releasing electro currents.

"Be at peace Lazar, no need to be afraid" the visitor replied.

"Here you need these, to help control it" the visitor handed Brother Dominick the Brown leather gloves, he had pulled out earlier from his chest of drawers.

"I...don't...understand" Brother Dominick was now on his bed, drowsy as his gloved hands were now at rest, he felt complete exhaustion coming from the early morning occurrences. The visitor said "It's time", then vanished... "impossible"

An hour later,

Brother Dominick heard a knock on the door loud enough to wake him up. "I'll be just a minute" he called out.

"All right, I'll be back in five minutes" He heard someone say.

While he was getting ready, he took the gloves off to wash, there were no emissions, "Thank God" Brother Dominick sighed in relief, but he was still uncertain of what it all meant and so he decided to put the gloves back on just to be on the safe side, as instructed by the mysterious horseman. He stepped out of the bedroom and was about to open his front door when suddenly it opened from the outside.

"Elder Enoch! Please come in" he invited the Elder inside a bit hurriedly, "something's wrong with me Elder," Brother Dominick said in full panic.

"Dominick, I saw..."

"You saw him? the man in my room didn't you, the same guy you spoke to that day in the woodlands" Brother Dominick was speaking with much urgency.

"Dominick, listen to me son, you need to calm down, get ahold of yourself before getting out of this room"

"What do you mean?" Brother Dominick asked him.

Elder Enoch placed both hands on his shoulders, suddenly Brother Dom felt absolute peace, his breathing was now at ease. "How did he do that?"

Elder Enoch faced him.

"Look at me Dominick" He waited until Brother Dominick's eyes were now fixated on him.

"You have been given a precious treasure, a unique ability that will help many, shh...let me finish" he added as Brother Dominick was about to speak. "Listen to me son and pay attention, I don't know what happened to you at the pine woodlands four days ago, but this is all connected, as you can see starting from your unexpected move from Europe to here"

"I'm not sure what this is all about, why me? I just want to serve and please him" Brother Dominick replied

"There lies the great mystery son, those words serving and pleasing, you didn't know what that entails, neither did I."

"I don't know what to do from here Elder Enoch."

"You'll know what to do, It'll come naturally."

"But how_."

"Your prayers have just been answered, but not necessarily

the way you expected" Elder Enoch replied, interrupting him.

"That says a great deal about how he sees you and what he wants from you" Elder Enoch paused still staring and Brother Dominick waited for him to finish; as he was very curious about what the Elder was saying.

"Last piece of advice son" Elder Enoch loosened his grip on Brother Dom's shoulders ready to leave the room.

"Be careful with those hands of yours, hold on to those special gloves..."

"Yeah, I definitely will Elder Enoch."

"No, you don't understand, what I mean is Eph 6:5 is happening to you, not everyone reacts the way I did, when they see a fellow human being with electric bolts shooting out of their hands like a comic book superhero...it could get dangerous, for you and those around you" Elder Enoch replied

"Sure, thanks Elder, no pressure," Brother Dominick said.

Elder Enoch chuckled at his reply "not to worry Dominick, just be opened and remember to whom much is given, much is required, it's called responsibility and maturity in the things of our Lord" then he said "Be discreet"

"Before you go, I have a question."

"Sure, what is it?"

"Who are you Elder Enoch?" Brother Dominick couldn't help but ask, he's always felt something very unusual and off about the Elder like he was not from around here, he thought honestly

"And back to your usual inquisitive self, I see" Elder Enoch smiled amused and added,"You have a visitor."

Just a few seconds after Elder Enoch mentioned a visitor, both men looked the door as a firm, quiet knock sounded.

A brother working in hospitality peeked inside the room.

"Good morning" he nodded.

"Elder Enoch" he greeted him surprised to see him standing in the room.

"Hello, Brother Oliver" Elder Enoch replied greeting the man who looked even much more surprised that the well-respected Elder knew him by name among the thousands of brothers in the monastery.

"Later Son, I have things to tend to at the chapel."

Brother Dominick nodded with full gratitude as Elder Enoch exited the room.

"There's someone here to see you Dominick" Brother Oliver said.

"Who is it? Did they give a name?' Brother Dominick had no idea who it could be because he never gets "visits" and never has during his entire journey in the monastic life.

Brother Oliver looked at a piece of paper he held in his hand and read the name out loud to him.

"Uh, a certain Commissioner Kinkade Takoda..."

Brother Oliver replied as they both stepped out of the room into the corridor, Brother Dominick froze, oh no Kinkade is... trouble... on a very large scale and the last person he expected to come to see him at the monastery.

"Good to see you have family coming to visit," Brother Oliver said as he was heading the opposite direction from Brother Dominick "wait how do you know he's family."

"He said you and him are related, best friends_" he replied observing Brother Dominick, finding him a bit out of sort.

"Is everything ok Dominick?" Brother Oliver asked.

"Yes, I'm fine, I'll go see him, thanks Oliver" The Latter nodded and walked away.

CHAPTER 5

SONS OF BOLT

BROTHER DOMINICK WALKED a few steps and stops abruptly as he sees someone standing in his path, on the way to the outer courtyard.

"Pazz Lazar Takoda, the one, and only" Kinkade called out from the short distance with his booming voice, Brother Dominick squinted his eyes with suspicion,

"Oh, my sincere apologies cousin, tsk...slip of the tongue... where are my manners, I meant to say 'Brother Dominick'" there was brief silence.

"Hello cousin, what brings you to our monastery?"

"Wow, so I need an official reason to visit my best friend..."

"I know you, Kinkade."

"Hmm, is that right?" He asked then looked at his cousin for a brief moment

"Walk with me Lazar" They began walking toward the East gate into the pine woodlands.

"Aunt Rachel asked about you, she's worried..."

"Tell mom, I'm okay"

"You haven't called for three weeks now"

"I'll call her, just...tell her not to worry I'm fine."

"What exactly brings you here Kinkade?"

His cousin was recently promoted to the rank of Commissioner after years in the police force, and prior to that, a short impactful time in the Navy, discharged with honor and he received more medals than one can imagine.

Since their childhood Kinkade has always been put in charge of looking after him, with Kinkade being five years older than Dominick, the family always had given him the title and task of big brother but he had never fully stepped into the role.

As a result, they were more like best friends...that is, until that one day, eight years ago when Brother Dominick announced to everyone that he found his purpose within the monastic life of the Brotherhood, to serve the Lord, the family was shocked and happy for him but Kinkade became a different person that day onward, he took the title of older Brother on another level.

As a very successful well to do man, Kinkade already had all the resources at his disposal to begin a secret investigation into the silver monastery of the Aegean Sea, and what he discovered was considered by him, arguments that would bring Brother Dominick into reason. But Dominick at the time refused to disobey or abort his calling off of his cousin's suspicions, there were no communications between them since that day, as Brother Dominick was aware of his cousin's extreme personality.

He was glad Kinkade's parents had sent him to military school early on, keeping him from causing more trouble than they could handle, he, of course, went on and was awarded a special warfare operator naval rating and navy enlisted classification after graduating from a navy seal 24-week BUD/S school and settled down with his wife Maia and two kids.

Brother Dominick was happy for the man his older cousin turned out to be, but knew Kinkade well enough to realize how much of a trouble maker he could be, when it came to him meddling in the affairs of the monastery and he knew that Kinkade did his homework on him, before coming to visit.

"You know little brother, I never understood why you had to leave everything and all of us behind to embrace this life" Kinkade asked, as they stood in the middle of the pine woodlands, Kinkade picked a rose lily from the nearby flower shrub, closed his eyes as he brought it to his strong blade of a nose to smell it. He then looked around him with keen admiration of nature, he treated his surrounding with care and respect, one looking from a distance would easily observe that commissioner Kinkade was enjoying the peaceful bliss of the pine woodlands.

"I'm not your little brother and _"

"Oh, but you are, and according to Takoda Tribe, I must

look after you" He replied with his black eyes staring at him.

"I think you really need some strong deliverance from that Hero complex of yours."

Kinkade looked at his cousin, with a serious face and his wide mouth that was forever edged with irreverent humor, he chuckled in genuine amusement, contrary to the intimidating countenance he presented with his unusual height and brawn, Kinkade always had a keen sense of humor to go along with his high intellect.

"Well thank you for your concern, Lazar, we'll look into my hero complex later, for now since you avoided the first question about why you chose this life_."

"It's my calling, my purpose to serve the Lord, I don't know how else to explain."

"You could have served many other ways, joining a good church, going on missions and so forth, going out on the streets, doing missionary work, but you chose to seclude yourself into...this..." he raised his hands towards his surroundings for emphasis.

"I could have this chat with you for hours and never expect you to understand..." Brother Dominick paused, suddenly he took a closer look at their surroundings and realized they ended up at the very location of the cabin where his strange encounter with the thunderbolt man took place, except where the cabin was days ago, was now and empty land with very short grass in its place, and his troublesome cousin was standing right in the center of that patch of land. Brother Dominick asked softly with much suspicion

"Kinkade, why are you here? Why are we here in this spot?"

"Are you aware that your official transfer transcript from the Aegean Sea to this cloister, mysteriously disappeared a day before your arrival?"

Brother Dominick had no idea but he hid his surprised expression.

"Why are you telling me this?"

"Oh nothing, just wanted to bring this to your attention."

"And you know this how?"

"All I'm doing is looking out for you little brother"

He noticed since childhood how Brother Dominick would get annoyed every time Kinkade called him 'Little Brother', so he's always relished himself in it, and today was the case, Kinkade smiled, completely amused by Brother Dominick's exasperated expression.

"You have absolutely no idea what you're getting yourself into, word of advice Big Brother, be careful"

"Aha!! So, there is something going on here, and I'm getting myself into it, hmm interesting"

Brother Dominick turned around and started walking away shaking his head

"Bolt...bolts of electricity ...lightning bolt" Kinkade said out loud.

Brother Dominick felt his heartbeat strongly against his chest, as he stopped in his tracks, he turned around back in Kinkade's direction and saw that his cousin had crouched down on the ground, the specific terrain where the cabin of the man of the lightning bolt was previously.

At that moment Brother Dominick understood that his cousin knew much more than he had realized

"But how?" he thought.

Brother Dom walked up to him slowly, where he had crouched down.

"Did you know that in order for thunder to form, clouds must be present?" Kinkade paused as he stood, hands in his pocket, and was observing his surrounding with a close focus on the ground, then he looked up at the sky all the while Brother Dominick was quiet, trying to figure out where Kinkade was going with this observation.

"Under the right conditions and with enough moisture, we would see big tall cumulonimbus clouds become amazing factories that make thunder, rain, and guess what? they even make bolts of electricity..." Kinkade paused and Brother Dominick felt his cousin wasn't done.

"what's this all about?" he asked.

Kinkade held up his hand to Dominick, in a gesture telling him to hold his thought.

He continued on, with both hands behind his back now, and went on explaining.

"Inside those clouds there are tiny crystals and water droplets moving around, hitting against each other, creating friction that as a result, it builds energy and generate sparks"

"Ok...and to what do I owe this great session of science 101?"

"There were reports of unusual weather activity four

days ago..."

"Kinkade, I have no idea what you're getting at, but the weather is one of the most predictable and also unpredictable occurrences to take place on a daily basis, we all know that."

Kinkade shook his head "No this is different, consecutive sequences of electric discharges between the atmosphere and the ground took place that day."

Both men looked at each other in silence for a moment.

"You know, that sounds all exciting, but I don't see how that has anything to do with you coming to see me"

"On that day there were no clouds in the sky, no rain or semblance of rain, it was all sunny around 4,5 in the morning...when suddenly...it happened...a trail of cloud to ground dry lightning along with thunder manifested out of nowhere and striking in multipattern, traveled in a specific direction all the way here, as its termination point, don't you find that a bit odd?"

"Very interesting indeed"

"Now tell me, Lazar, you are a man of God, tell me the truth, did you personally witness these electro waves coming from the sky?" More silence.

"I think we're done here, Kinkade."

"Rumors are going around that you've been visiting the pine woodlands quite a bit lately, that's why I'm asking you, little brother."

"Wow, you go off of rumors circulating now? Come on cousin you can do better than that."

"Refusing to admit the truth then diverting is as much as admitting the truth entirely," He chuckled.

"Listen, I'm all right Kinkade, you really don't need to meddle into monasteries matters," Brother Dominick tried to reassure him.

"Ahh Pazz Lazar but I'm only getting warmed up I promised the Eagle I would do all I can to look after you and protect this family."

"Don't do that, don't use my dad, your uncle as a means to satiate your own personal quest of the Ego."

"Is that what you think I'm doing? It doesn't matter, your dad, the Eagle's favor he asked of me a week before his passing...he asked me in confidence to specifically look after you, and I intend to make sure on that promise."

"You're not my guardian angel."

He smiled "of course not, I'm your big brother Lazar, that's that, there are many things...going on in this place you call monastery, and I intend to find out, to protect you."

"If I renounce the monastic life, would you stop your investigation?" Brother Dominick asked.

"Ha! Yeah right, nice try Lazar, I know you better than you think, it might as well start raining pink elephants" Kinkade laughed.

"Speaking of which, I have to get Sarya her pink giraffe from the toy shop or I'm in trouble."

Brother Dominick sighed in relief as they began walking back into the cathedral's gates.

"Something or I should say many things, strange,

unexplainable happened to you that day Lazar...trust me I can tell, there's something different about you and mark my words...I intend to uncover everything."

"You're on your own then."

"Don't worry, you're better looked after when you're not involved little brother" Kinkade replied as they arrived at the main entrance.

"Monastic business aside, I am glad to see you Pazz Lazar" He gave brother Dominick a solid arm shake.

"what's this?" Brother Dom felt something in his hand as he shook hands with Kinkade...a gold-tone bald eagle metal figurine medal.

"a small gift, the eagle gave it to me and now you can have it"

"No, I can't take this, thank you I truly am, touched but it's against protocol, why don't you keep it for me."

"No, I insist, just you keep it for me, as a gift, a temporary one" they both laughed.

"Ok will do and thanks Kinkade."

"For what?"

"Coming to visit, I'll call mom, I won't forget."

"Ok, keep in touch, but anyway I'm coming back here much sooner than you think, in a week to be exact."

Brother Dom shook his head exasperated.

"Why are you doing this?"

"Talk to you later little brother, some fancy gloves you got there," Kinkade replied as he exited the monastery deliberately not answering his questions.

As commissioner Kinkade left, Brother Dominick whispered “and here we go” he said to himself sighing, then walked away...completely oblivious to the two men who stepped out of the shadows, both facing the direction where Brother Dominick left.

“The commissioner will be back sir,” Brother Oliver said “in three days’ time” he added.

“Good, we’ve been waiting for him, secure a meeting with Priest Superior for me, cancel out the rest of the day” Elder Enoch replied.

Brother Oliver nodded and walked away not knowing what the Elder meant by waiting for him.

Indeed, commissioner Kinkade Takoda was completely unaware of what awaited him in the days ahead.

CHAPTER 6

TASTE PRIMAVERA

"GREAT! —FINALLY MADE it" Victoria looked around the room, then the rest of the small cottage, booked for her entire stay at the Colorado wood pines.

"Yay!! I'm so excited for you Vee, and it looks like Bandjo is too, aren't you little fella"

Isa-Elle's voice and Bandjo's barks could be heard from Victoria's phone

"So have you met the team yet?"

"I'm meeting them in half an hour, wait oh no I'm running late! gotta go Isa-Elle, love ya"

"Call you later Hun, love you!"

"Ok now, step one get ready, step two double check I brought everything, step three meet the team," Victoria told herself.

"Now I sound like a lunatic talking to myself" she

chuckled as she stepped outside.

It was full spring, and the weather combined with nature all around gave it a heavenly feel.

Victoria breathed in and out slowly, then headed to the closest park where she is to meet the team,

"Excuse me, miss! Excuse me!" Victoria turned around as she heard the sound of a young girl calling.

"Can you help me, please? I kinda got lost" the girl said.

"of course, come with me" Victoria always loved children, she's volunteered in child care centers, babysitting, even filled in as an English substitute teacher in an elementary school once even though she didn't have all the required credentials at that time.

The little girl looked to be no more than nine years old.

"What's your name princess?" the girl extended her hand, Victoria reached out, then holding hands they began walking toward the park where Victoria was sure to get help from the team, a team she has yet to meet with, they walked quietly and she had enough experience, with children, she knew the little one will eventually tell her name when she felt comfortable, she must have been with someone close by who is now looking for her.

"Kayla, my name's Kayla" the little girl finally answered.

"What a pretty name for a beautiful girl" the girl smiled .

"I know, thank you!" Victoria laughed.

"Oh, look miss! Look!"

"Call me Victoria."

“Victoria look, a bunny!” Kayla started running after it.

“Wait! Kayla...wait for me!” Victoria ran after the excited little girl, finally catching up to her, she saw her standing still, staring at a small hole in the ground by a rosebush.

“it’s gone, oh well, can you take me back now?’

“Sure, let’s go.”

They walked a brief distance and finally Victoria sees a group of adults and a group of children standing by Park benches and tables.

“Don’t worry, we’ll find your parents.”

“Oh, I’m not with my parents, I’m here with my teachers and my class.”

“Really? That must be them over there, I’m guessing” Victoria pointed at a group of Children.

“And what do you know Kayla, that’s my team!” Victoria was surprised because her ‘team’ seemed somehow affiliated with the children’s group, she had no idea what the trip was about except exploring the nearby nature wonder.

“Victoria, I presume?” a young man in mid-twenties greeted her as Kayla and her both arrived at the park.

“Hi yes, how are you? Sorry I’m late, I also brought Kayla with me, she got lost on the way” Victoria realized she just managed to state five different matters all in one sentence thinking she must be a bit too nervous.

“Oh awesome, I’m Simon by the way, the supervisor” they both shook hands.”

“Nice to meet you Simon.”

"Cool Victoria and no worries you didn't miss much, so we are a group of teachers, of all kinds from various domain from Botanist, mathematicians, chemist, English teachers to drama teachers, also astronauts, etc." Simon stayed quiet, pausing with an amused expression on his face, he looked at Victoria as if expecting some type of reaction.

Victoria looked at him with eyebrows raised then understood he just made a joke and tried to see if she caught it.

"Ah astronauts huh? That was a good one" she chuckled.

Simon laughed and nodded toward the rest of the team.

"All right let me introduce you to the others, come on," Victoria walked over to the group of adults and saw Kayla among the children telling the story about her exciting meet and greet with a bunny to another young boy who she thought might be either her best friend or her brother, she was talking with animated gestures describing her day.

Victoria was introduced to everyone on her team, she was teamed up with a physicist named Dr. Zahid Hassan whom she will be assisting with two kids assigned under him, he was also a science teacher.

Dr Zahid was known to have a passionate heart for all things science-physics and the wonders of traditional cuisine, Victoria was humorously told by Simon.

"What's the name of the school who put this whole trip together?" Victoria asked Simon.

"It's more like an idea that a group of teachers, myself included, within Eagle County got together from different schools and approached the Board of Education, regarding the need for children to get away from their electronics like tablets, televisions, video games and step outside more to learn about science in nature along with its mysteries."

"Wow, that's an amazing initiative, how does it work exactly? How do the children get selected?"

"They're picked at random, what I mean is, there's a simple system behind it that our small research team would know more about, but the main objectives and goals were consolidated...well you would call it an acrostic if it were a Poem."

"Oh really? Interesting, so what's the Acrostic?"

"All right, so we compressed our objectives and plans of what we hope to achieve together with the children as a team and named it...this," Simon walked over to a black chalkboard, Victoria didn't realize was there, white chalk in hand, he started writing:

Project Exodus

E
Xplore
X
O bserve
D iscover
U nite
S olve

Wow, that's amazing Simon, I admire what you guys are doing for your community and I'm honored to be a part of this, this will be fun."

"Oh yes it will, the kids will love it, now here's a map of your team's destination and what to explore, yes, I know, before you say it Victoria, I took into account your specific interest in the mount of the Holy Cross and guess what? since you're here on a volunteering basis... we were able to place you with Dr. Zahid's team who's assigned to the areas between the shrine pass and the mount of the Holy cross."

"Thank you soo much!" Victoria interrupted him full of excitement.

"...as a sign of our gratitude" Simon laughed finishing the rest of his sentence.

"And by all means, you're very welcome."

"Allright, I have to head to the front to address the entire group, as we're about to start dispatch here soon."

"Ok no problem thanks!" Victoria replied.

Simon nodded and went on to give instructions to each team, the teams were named by a specific color, with the matching color badges and gear bags, when they were all ready, then everyone regrouped.

"Listen everyone, and of course I'm emphasizing more on the adults, I know some of the teachers here are also parents whose children are in Project Exodus" Simon said happily as he looked around at all the faces watching him.

"I'm really honored and humbled that you've selected, me to supervise this month's project Exodus once again."

"How about last month guys? Wasn't it amazing, our very first excursion" everyone clapped their hands excitedly, some whistles sounded.

"Ok I'll be going over the instructions on the colors and the rules, and then we should all get started then meet back up here in the park at 3:30 pm."

"The color you've been given is like the picture on your government ID card and the Hex Color code for that specific color would be similar to the ID number on our ID card or Driver's license..." Simon continued on.

"Each child you've been assigned to guide and chaperoned has a lanyard with a beeping badge around their neck in case they get lost, in an emergency or feel in danger, and if you're not close to them for some reason, they would press the button on the badge, and your wristband will start beeping..." He paused.

"Your wristbands are not regular wristbands as you can see, they look and function more like smartwatches and once it starts beeping, it has GPS capability, to show you where the child is" Simon looked at the group and saw that someone lifted their hand for a question.

"You have a question? Sure, go ahead."

"Hi everyone, I'm Mrs. Perry, just wondering, could this technology be implemented on our phones, like apps and such instead of having the bracelets or wristbands rather?"

"That's a great question Mrs. Perry, we could you're right, we've thought about it and found out that it was more within our budget from the board to create those wristbands and more importantly beepers; also, phones are not as reliable, when going on high altitude, terrain for example, there could be loss of signal and such" She nodded saying thanks.

"Any other question so far? Ok" he continued on.

"When the child presses the button, the color's corresponding Hex Color code will come up on the wristband's screen as authentication and also to make sure that there's no interference with our satellite for security purposes, verifying that the signal is secure, this all to ensure that the excursion goes well and everyone gets back safely having had an amazing experience ok?"

"I know that was a mouthful but the success of these excursions also depends on a good system set in place for all of us" Simon paused to drink his water then said.

"Oh, and one more thing, when the child presses the button, which by the way we've already gone over the button pressing with them, but you're more than welcome to reiterate with your children...as I was saying when the child presses it, both adults on the team will get the signal..."

"All righty! Done! Now let's have fun" everyone clapped and shouted.

Victoria was on Team Dark Terra Cotta, with Hexadecimal color code cc4ec.

Overall, on the Dark Terra Cotta team was Victoria Ruth, Dr. Zahid Hasan as teachers working with children Kayden and Kayla which she found out were brother and sister.

"They're twins actually" Dr. Zahid had said when she asked.

"You guys are ready?" He asked.

“Yess!” the children said, Victoria laughed.

Dr. Zahid had the GPS on in the car, their destination was about a fifteen minutes’ drive.

Victoria was excited about this whole journey, “Wait did I leave the stove on at the cottage,” she thought then Victoria caught herself “oh no I won’t do it this time, trying too hard to have unnecessary panics” she thought to herself humorously.

“Gonna be an amazing day” she took a deep breath.

“Yes, it will” Dr Zahid said smiling kindly, Victoria realized.

She said her last sentence out loud, she smiled back then looked in the back,

The twins were looking out the closed window, pointing at different objects of nature and animals they saw.

CHAPTER 7

A DIAMOND AND A ROSE

"IT LOOKS LIKE this must be the shrine pass toward the mount of the Holy Cross" Victoria said all excited.

"Are we here Victoria?" Kayden asked as they were walking between rows of flowers and grass, "Yeah we are here kids, but I just got a call from Simon."

Dr Zahid said then paused looking at Victoria.

"What did he say?" Victoria had a feeling this wouldn't sound good.

"He said the Holy Cross mount is currently blocked off by a construction site, he spoke to one of the officers on patrol, who told him there were unusual atmospheric occurrences some days ago resulting in the main road to the Holy cross being greatly damaged by lightning strikes.

"Lightning strikes? that's so strange, I hope no one got hurt" Victoria replied.

“Aww maan! So, what are we gonna do now?” Kayden asked.

“Hopefully it won’t be boring” Kayla told her brother.

“Me too kids, I hope not, I was really looking forward to this one” Victoria sighed.

“I’m sorry you all, I’m sure there must be some exciting places here to be able to explore this great landscape around us.”

“Oh, ohh I have a better idea Dr Zahid, I was thinking_”

“Wait Kayla, it was me who had that idea” Kayden said.

“Wha_! Ok fine you say it” Kayla replied with her arms crossed, both children definitely shared a family resemblance with their Dark caramel hues. Kayden’s reddish-brown dreads and Kayla puffed-up ponytail added to their unique beauty “making them absolutely adorable” Victoria thought smiling shaking her head at the sibling’s small bantering.

“All right soo, me and Kayla were picking those color rocks over there and then we saw someone, it was a man_”

“Now wait a minute, you saw a man? Where?” Dr. Zahid asked.

“Kids! Oh my God, you spoke to a stranger? You need to be very careful, what did he look like and what did he give you?”

“He is very nice, he works at the church, he was wearing this long blue shirt, it’s like way long, all the way down to his feet, I forgot what it’s called,” Kayden said.

"And look! He gave us these shiny rocks, he said uh he said that it's more fun inside the garden" Kayla replied.

"No wait, are you sure Kayla? I think he said um the maze? I think, yes the maze!" Kayden replied.

Victoria turned to face Dr Zahid "but I don't understand, how were they out of our sight long enough for them to go meet a stranger and come back to tell the story?" Victoria frowned in deep thought,

"You and Dr Zahid were looking at the phone, when Kayla and I went to that side over there to look at more rocks, and then this man told us about the garden and."

"And we could go play there or explore, isn't that cool, actually can we go see him?" Kayla said.

Victoria was very intrigued by the kid's tale of a man in a robe, when suddenly she stopped in her tracks.

"Oh, my goodness Dr Zahid! I think they're talking about a monastery close by."

"Ahh yes you're right, there is in fact a monastery around here...we must be very close for the man to have met the kids this close" he said.

"Kayla why you keep interrupting me, it's so annoying like for real" Kayden was whispering to his sister as they were walking with Victoria and their science teacher.

"Okay kids lets mend our differences before going any further into this path_"

"What does 'mend' mean?" Kayden asked.

"Interrupting much little mister? It means to fix

something" Victoria responded smiling shaking her head.

Kayla snickered a laugh as her brother was making funny faces at her.

"Ok kiddos, let's keep going, we don't have much time if we have to fill in the explorer's log before getting back to the park by 3:30 pm" Dr Zahid said.

And a few minutes later they arrived at a large wall with long rich foliage hanging all over it, so full that it would be hard to see where the entrance or door is if there was one present.

"Kids, is this where you saw him? The man" Victoria asked.

"Yes, he was here actually" Kayden said.

Kayla nodded in agreement then added "He came through the wall...I think"

Both adults looked at each other completely puzzled.

"No way, there must be an entrance here somewhere among the foliage" Victoria said.

Suddenly the group sees a squirrel hurry on out from the bottom of the foliage.

"There definitely must be an entrance, let's keep looking kids and _" Dr Zahid was saying

"Found it!" the twins shouted at the same time.

"you children are geniuses, aren't you?" Victoria said laughing pleasantly.

Dr Zahid told Victoria and the kids to stay behind him

and let him step through first.

It was in fact a wooden door camouflaged in the green foliage hanging on the wall. As they stepped inside suddenly Victoria felt a familiarity with the place but she didn't know why.

It was an entrance to what she now realized was a maze, Victoria was contemplating the arresting beauty of nature, as were the kids and Dr Zahid.

There was a silence, so peaceful and harmonious that it seems even the twitch of a finger could be heard.

Everyone was absorbed and distracted by the breathtaking beauty of the maze, lost in its surroundings. Victoria didn't notice and even feel someone coming out of the trees walking up behind her, with all the trees around them the bright sunlight only hit certain angles in and around the maze's entrance.

Victoria's heart beat a little stronger, she felt a sensation on her neck, like a feathered caress. She turned around while everyone else was still absorbed by nature all around the maze.

She suddenly came face to face with a man about 5 feet from each other or she knew it was a man but it was so dark, she couldn't make out the shape, or see anything clearly when suddenly her eyes focused on two, very minuscule flames horizontally suspended in the air at an equal distance from each other about six feet high, Victoria had lifted her head up to look at it in absolute astonishment, the small burning flames were close to each other, suspended side by side.

"You should take a look at this Victoria" Dr Zahid spoke out loud as he was walking toward her. Simultaneously Victoria was startled by the Dr's voice breaking her out of her frozen state, she turned around to look at him with such vivacity that she accidentally missed a step, lost momentum then was about to fall backward when she felt strong arms catch her from behind just in time.

"Victoria! Are you ok?" Dr Zahid walked quickly.

"Thank you, sir," he added, addressing the man who saved Victoria from falling backward.

"It's him! It's him!' Kayla said running toward them with Kayden in tow.

"Hi Elder Clem!" Kayden said.

"you're ok Victoria?" the man asked.

Victoria had turned around to look at him, she had to look up and couldn't believe her own eyes...of all the probabilities in the world this Elder Clem the children were so fond of, they were, in fact, hugging him at the hip with such genuine affection, he was none other than the mysterious stranger she met a week ago at the park in her neighborhood back home in Seattle.

He smiled at the kids and briefly kissed each twin on their heads affectionately. Strange enough the children somehow loved him as if they've known him their whole life. Kayden was asking him a question and he had stooped down to the kid's height to hear and answer their questions very patiently.

"Those colored rocks are not regular rocks Victoria, one

of the kids accidentally dropped them without noticing and as I picked them up, I noticed cracks on both due to the impact so I gently pressed them and I see these...inside, take a look."

Dr Zahid held up both hands to Victoria for her to see and right in the middle of both palms were...gems, one purple and the other blue.

"Oh my God...are they real?" Victoria asked surprisingly.

"I'm not sure but just by looking at it from a physicist's eye I'd say yes, but they're not part of the environment so to speak...they don't belong to the flora or biota of this place."

"Sorry, what do you mean?" Victoria said.

"What I mean is you won't find these gems lying around inside random rocks everywhere, it's impossible"

"So strange, although the kids will be excited to see what they've discovered for Project Exodus" Victoria said.

"Yes, they will be but see here's the thing Victoria, from what I recall the twins were saying they didn't 'discover' it... the shiny rocks they said_"

"The man in the long robe gave them those rocks..." Victoria whispered amazed and intrigued by his man who calls himself Elder Clem, what kind of name is that anyway" Victoria thought as she was readjusting her satchel, she happened to casually look up and paused startled, he was staring at her... the same way he did when he came and sat next to her at the bench park in Seattle. His unusual coffee brown eyes in contrast with his Dark blue robe.

The mysterious man looked at Victoria in such a manner

no one has ever looked at her this way...like he wanted something far more complicated from her, she quickly lowered her gaze. He was walking with the twins toward them.

"Elder Clem, the children mentioned a garden within the maze that would be a great place for them to explore?" Dr Zahid asked.

"Absolutely, it'd be my pleasure, follow me" Elder Clem responded then he walked ahead of them, toward the maze entrance, which must have been one of the many entrances, as Victoria notices one other big entry point similar to the one they came from, on the far end. This was a big and extensive maze she noticed.

Dr Zahid was very intrigued by Elder Clem since the discovery of the gems inside stones, with a physicist's enthusiasm, he was now walking next to the Elder, asking him questions respectfully and she on purpose stayed behind with the twins, walking a bit slower. Victoria felt odd around the mysterious man, as she tried to call him Elder Clem but found herself reverting back to mysterious man, she had a strong feeling the Elder was not who he said he was, and there was much more to him than he let on, the robe and title were a disguise, she was sure of it.

He was powerful with this unique authoritative air, that gave him away as someone high in leadership, even though he was trying to hide it with much genuine humility.

Arms folded behind his back he walked calmly with Dr Zahid. Victoria felt drawn to him and all that he was. The same unfamiliar impressions she felt at the bench park a week ago, of feeling belonged to… "he's dangerous" so she decided it be best to avoid any interactions with him while in the garden "the faster we do this, the faster I go back to the hotel and call Isa-Elle asap and back to normal life" she thought.

"Here we are everyone" Elder Clem spread out his hands pointing at the surroundings,

"Woow! This is soooo cool!!" Kayden exclaimed.

"I know right! Thank you Elder Clem! Let's go Kayden hurry, I'll check here" Kayla said.

"And I'll check over there, wow look at those flowers" Kayden said.

"They're called hydrangeas" Elder Clem said.

"What about these?" Kayla asked holding white flowers.

"Those are Easter Lilies" both kids were excited and sat down on the ground to write down their reports for Project Exodus and go on for more discoveries.

"This is a magnificent garden and it's quite big"

Dr Zahid told the Elder as they progressed not far from where the children were. He nodded at the Dr's comment smiling then said "there's a variety on this side, along with my favorite…"

Victoria came closer out of curiosity, she wanted to see, she looked behind her and was surprised to see that Dr Zahid wasn't there, he stayed behind looking at another flower species, and keeping an eye on the twins who were now closer to him chitchatting about the number of small animals they saw so far around the garden.

"Dr Zahid! Are you coming?"

"He's on his way" Elder Clem replied.

Victoria felt her heart skip a beat, she turned around to face him and sees that he was using floral snips to cut the most beautiful, large Red Rose she's ever seen, once done, he took the rose and handed it to her...she looked at him not knowing what to do, hesitating for a moment, she carefully accepted the rose, then she felt somehow there was more meaning to his gesture, she remembered the strange occurrences of the Rose and rose petals, she had back home all the while, he was looking at her...

A nice fresh breeze suddenly wafted into the garden's atmosphere, complementing, Victoria couldn't help but breathe in and breathe out. "Beautiful day isn't?" she heard him say.

She quickly looked at him and saw that he hadn't spoken out loud instead it was his voice in her mind, "impossible" she thought, there was something odd with his eyes, their color resembled very much dark brown to terracotta, the color code name of her Project Exodus team, was it pure coincidence? she was confused, the more she discovered about him and the more she felt to steer clear from him.

Victoria took a step back still holding the rose he gave her, with both hands. He once again had that same expression in his eyes, as he now turned his complete attention away from the roses and to her. "Flaming, orange brown" she thought amazed.

"I'm sorry for taking so long Victoria, I had to get the twins work wrapped up, I think our time's up, we have to get back" Dr Zahir walked up to them, unaware of what had transpired.

Victoria let her breath out, not realizing she was holding it at some point. Thankful for the interruption and not to appear uncourteous, she whispered. "Thank you for the tour" walking away hurriedly. Dr Zahid shook the Elder's hand, "thank you, the twins are happy with how their project turned out" he said, Elder Clem nodded, smiling.

"Let me show you the way out" he replied.

"Ah yes that would be great thank you" Dr Zahid said.

As they all headed out guided by Elder Clem toward the maze's exit, and unto the location, they came from originally, Victoria realized they would have been completely lost without being shown the way, "this maze is one of the hardest to figure out" she thought. Dr Zahid shook hands once again with Elder Clem, the twins hugged him, as they were all stepping out of an entry point. He was standing at the entrance greeting each one saying farewell.

Victoria was the last to come to the entrance she looked up and said "goodbye" politely, wanting to leave as quickly as she could.

"See you soon Victoria..." the Elder was holding a small round reddish colored stone the size of a nickel and placed it inside her rose.

Victoria had little time to react to his response and what he placed inside the crevasses of the rose.

He smiled, all perfect white teeth showing. He had this strange ability to draw her into communicating with him just with a simple stare, letting her know what he wanted from her. Victoria's sense of preservation was on high alert, she was aware of him being much more than a normal man, and was determined to stay far from the complexities of this mysterious man of the red rose "see you...very soon... Victoria" He on purpose said the words slowly to add emphasis.

Victoria walked quickly to join her team then looked back to see that he was gone in a split second from her looking back, she sighed in relief.

"There you are Victoria! Let's go! I'm so excited!" Kayla said.

"Kayla shows me your explorer bag and I'll show you mine" Kayden said.

"Ok!" Kayla replied and the kids were animatedly talking about the amazing experience of Project Exodus and how they can't wait to tell their parents and older siblings.

"Victoria, is everything ok with you? You seemed quite perturbed in the garden." Dr Zahid asked as they were driving back to the park.

"No, no I'm fine, just a bit tired from the journey." Victoria tried to find a believable excuse to tell the Dr Zahid.

"Hmm, this Elder...there's something quite peculiar about him, not only threatening, but powerful at the same time, don't you think?" Dr Zahid asked looking at her with his sideway glances, trying to study her reaction.

Victoria knew what he was trying to do, she made an effort to cover her emotions even more as she responded.

"Yeah, I think so in a way, he was just a little too much into his flowers though" she chuckled trying to lighten the mood.

"Yes, you're right" Dr Zahid replied smiling then focused fully on the road.

Hours later, Victoria was back in her room at the cottage speaking with her best friend Isa-Elle on facetime. "You know what Isa-Elle, from time to time, he would have this expression in his eyes, it's like he wants something from me, and whatever that is, I just know it's much more complicated and foreign to me...I don't get it."

"Whoa, I'm still trying to process the part where you said this Elder Clem is the exact same person as the mysterious man of the Red rose you met at the Park here."

She shook her head in amazement, then she continued on "by the way did you look at that stone in the rose yet?"

"No not yet, let me do that now actually."

Victoria took a long rectangular-shaped jewelry box, she opened it and pulled the rose out, she then replaced the container with a vertical standing glass dome, and retrieved the stone out of the rose afterward, she placed the rose back in the glass dome container.

"This glass case makes me think of beauty and the beast" Isa-Elle said laughing.

"Oh yeah you're right, didn't even think of that" Victoria replied smiling.

She then took the rock and holding it between her thumb and index finger, she hit it hard on the wooden chest by her bed, and looked at it for any cracks, she saw a small crack at the center, she hit it harder this time with a loud sound.

"Watch out for those fingers Vee."

"Yess, finally it cracked open, now let's see what's inside..."

Victoria gasped, eyes wide in shock.

"Oh no wait a minute, Vee, is that really what I think it is?...is that a_"

"Diamond..." Victoria finished her friend sentence with a whisper, she sat still on her bed looking at a large round radiant diamond like it was one of the seven wonders of the world.

"Earth to Victoria!" her friend called out,

Victoria snapped back "Sorry, I just, I..." frowning deep in thought, trying to decipher the meaning and the implications behind this.

"This mysterious man of the Red Rose placed a diamond inside a stone, inside a Rose...this is getting super weird Victoria"

"And he said, something to me, he said he would see me very soon and I don't know what that means or what to do. I'd rather avoid him. And you know what else? he is so... raw in his approach, intimidating even in the way he looks at me with his eyes, yet I'm so drawn to him and ..."

"And what Victoria?"

"I have a feeling; he is not quite human."

“Well double duh!!, the man is super powerful, he can appear and disappear, not to mention he’s richer than Croesus, with superpowers manifesting precious stones out of his bare hands”

“No, I mean yes you’re right but there’s something else that happened at the maze inside the monastery”

“Oh really? What happened and you can tell me anything, you know that right?”

“Yes of course, ok so at first, we went in with Dr Zahid and the kids just looking at nature around us, I mean you should have seen it Isa-Elle, it was out of this world when suddenly, I felt a tender touch on my neck, I mean weightless like a feather sat on my neck then lifted with the wind” she paused remembering that moment, Isa-Elle was quiet, listening carefully. “Then I turned around to see what it was, I strongly felt the presence of a man, He was right in front of me face to face, but it was so dark in that part of the maze by the trees, I couldn’t see clearly”

“But even if, it was dark, don’t you think you would still be able to see him, or hear him breathing for example” Isa-Elle replied.

“Yes, you’re right but here’s the weird part, I could feel it, I could make out a silhouette, that’s how I know it was a man but yet I couldn’t see him with clear eye view so to speak” Isa-Elle nodded, waiting for her to go on.

“Then suddenly in the blink of an eye, I see two minuscule burning flames suspended in the air.”

“Wow.”

"I tried to squint my eyes; I didn't dare to come any closer because I had absolutely no clue what that was."

"To be honest with you Hun here's how I see it...I think those flames are somehow connected to this Elder Clem slash mystery man of the Red Rose, and Victoria...sorry to say but our vibrant and charismatic superpowered-superrich-superman seemed to have taken a strong, invested interest in you, way before you even knew it"

"Wait what do you mean way before?"

"Well, he came after you in the park...how did he find you? How did he know where you were? How did it all start? Then himself or one of his strongmen mysteriously appeared at your place more than once...since then he has managed to communicate with you and place a personal marking on you by way of the rose...hmmm one can only wonder what he wants from you, I would want to find out if I were you..."

"Oh no no no, see that's where you and I are different, I don't want to find out, I don't want abnormal super-mega anything...I would like to get back to ways of normalcy, where things actually make sense..."

"Hmm...really? You're not even intrigued just a little?" Isa-Elle asked with suspicion in her voice

"Ok maybe just a little but-"

"So, you're not even interested to at least, put that rose and large diamond you're holding under a microscope in a manner of speaking and..."

"Wait! What d'you just say?" Victoria was walking around

her room and stopped.

"Umm I said a lot of things, I said."

"You said microscope!"

"Yeah…so… what do you mean?"

"Wait hold on, sorry I'm getting a call from…Simon? Of all people" Victoria found it unusual that Simon from Project Exodus was calling.

"Ok you go ahead; I'll go grab something in the kitchen but let's stay on facetime"

"Yeah, no problem, I have you on my tablet" Victoria said then answered the call

"Hey Simon, how are you?"

"Hi Victoria, I hope you had fun today and got back ok."

"Yes, it was a great, once in a lifetime experience definitely and yes I'm at the Hotel, my flight back home is tomorrow."

"That's great to hear, all right I'm not gonna take up much of your time, just had a question for you, when I called Dr Zahid to let you guys know about the Holy Cross mount being closed, where exactly did you go?"

Victoria had Simon on speaker as she was walking around the living room moving the tablet over.

"Uh well we followed the shrine pass path all the way to a certain spot." She said then waited for his response.

"Simon?…Simon are you there?"

"Yes, I'm here, sorry…. I'm just checking something and I'll tell you what it's all about in just a minute, Victoria can you first answer a question for me?"

"Sure."

"What exactly was the spot you alluded to earlier, can you do your best to describe it to me please?"

"This is getting weirder" she thought.

"So, after your call with Dr Zahid, we honestly didn't know where to go or to start...Dr. Zahid suggested that we just do our best and explore the shrine pass itself, but the kids had another idea and said that they had gone a little further into the shrine pass and found this place, while the Dr and I were looking at the map on his phone..."

"Yes? go on please, in detail if as best as you can."

"So, we followed them to see where they went, we kept walking straight down the shrine pass until we came in front of this wall with massive foliage...there was a hidden door practically camouflaged by the massive green foliage we opened it and found ourselves in the North entrance of a maze, that belongs to a monastery...now can you tell me please what's going on, I'm getting a little worried...did we do something wrong? Something happened...?"

"No, no not at all, you're fine, Team Dark Terracotta was successful with Project Exodus...it's not about the project itself per se, it's about that specific location of the wall with foliage containing a camouflaged door..."

"What about it?" Victoria said very intrigued.

"Well, we couldn't pick it up from our satellite...until a specific point in time."

"I'm sorry Simon can you please explain what that means?"

"Ok that means I will have to show it to you in person, do you think, there's time you could meet me at the park we were in earlier? Say in about half an hour? If that's possible?"

"Yes of course, I'm really interested to know, all right see you then" the line disconnected.

"whoah! What's going on? Isa-Elle I'm not sure I'm prepared to hear what he's about to tell me."

"Well first of all, I'm prepared, so hear it as if I'm there with you best friend, and second...Hun, you'll get tired of hearing me say this but whatever he tells you, one thing I know for sure...It's all directly connected to the mysterious Elder Clem of the Red Rose."

Victoria sighed "I was afraid you'd say that...and you even cleaned up your title naming I see" she said laughing at the way her best friend referred to the mystery man.

"Yep, that's about right" Isa-Elle laughed.

Then added "oh wait before I let you go can you tell me real quick what you meant by microscope?"

"Oh yeah, I have an idea, but I'll tell you when I see you at home tomorrow."

"Gotcha, ok I might not call back later but I'll call you sometime tomorrow or call me when you arrive at the airport."

"Sounds good, see ya later."

CHAPTER 8

SIMON SAYS...

VICTORIA GOT READY then headed for the park, she arrived on time and saw Simon standing by a table and bench with his laptop and a few documents on the table.

"Hey Victoria, thanks for coming," she noticed that Simon looked both excited and perturbed, she wasn't sure if it was a good or bad thing.

"Hi Simon, thank you for wanting to share this with me when you weren't obliged to."

"Oh, it's ok, you're welcome, I think somehow I felt that you should know about this for some reason, I couldn't explain why," Simon said as they sat down.

"Ok so let's get straight to it...so the Board of Education is like a big fan of Project Exodus, to the point where they were the ones who came up with the idea of acquiring a satellite for it, in fact it was one board member who's a wife and a mother that first mentioned it, the board liked it and months later, here we are…" He smiled then continued on.

"We name our satellite Exodus of course, so if you take a look at the screen, you'll see here our software that runs the satellite, the smart people who created it, made it easy for satellite illiterate like myself, to be able to read them easily in the form of a map," Simon explained with humor, smiling as Victoria chuckled.

"Then I consider myself a satellite illiterate as well" she replied playfully.

"Well, you won't be in the next minute once I explain further, so pay attention please," he said kindly

"You're ready? Ok now the teacher's wristband that you and Dr Zahid had on, has GPS capability that timestamps every time when you both arrive at one specific location, then it records the amount of time you spent at that location…lets call it location A. It records the time you arrive at location A then when you physically leave that location, it also records it and it reads in minutes, you're following me so far?"

"Yes, I get it," Victoria answered briefly allowing him to go on.

"So, the wristbands allow us to calculate the time span between your arrival at location A and your departure from that location, it gives us a total number of minutes spent at that place, and by leaving or arriving, I mean it doesn't matter what means of travel, you could be walking on foot or by car driving, it can read it just fine…and the same concept goes with the children's beepers, the timestamp is displayed on the beeper's screen."

Victoria nodded, fully alert and attentive.

Simon continued on "the instrument's function and usage I explained to you so far are for the teacher and the child in Project Exodus, now what I'm about to explain to you is how the data recorded on the wristbands and beeper reads on our satellite screen..."

"When I was looking at the records of Dark Terracotta... your team timespan and usage, I noticed incredible and impossible realities...ok here it is I printed out the time record to show it to you, so now you'll be both a spectator and participant in this presentation...here can you read these timespan data to me? I'm making a point so please bear with me K?"

Victoria took the paper he handed her then began to read out loud:

Team Dark Terracotta

For Project Exodus

Time spent at foliage according to:
**Dr Zahid Hassan wristband readings:*

22 minutes
**Victoria Ruth Wristband readings:*
22 minutes
**Children's Individual beeper readings:*
Showing two entries:

For Kayden's beeper:
2.2 minutes
Second reading:
22 minutes
Total time spent for Kayden: 24.2 minutes

For Kayla's beeper:
2.2 minutes
Then a second reading:

22 minutes
Total time spent for Kayla: 24.2 minutes.

Signed by

Simon Peter

"Before we go on, umm your name is Simon Peter?" Victoria asked amusedly

"Yeah, I know, I get that a lot my last name's Peter so my parents are Christians, we all are so they thought it'll be cool to have a Simon Peter in the Peter family tree and so they named me Simon, just imagine how my life has been, dealing with my school teachers back then and my college professors afterward then again, my colleagues at work... let just say I made it to fame status at this point" Simon comedic elaboration made Victoria's whole body genuinely shake with mirth.

"I'm sorry Simon but I really don't even feel bad for you

right now, I started at first but then all my compassion evaporated."

Victoria was saying in between crying laughter as Simon chuckled.

"Well, ok so anyway I see the timespan here- "

"Hold on Victoria before you tell me your observation let me lay out one more fact or I should say data...the satellite readings, ok I'm going to be talking a bit longer so just be ready k?" she nodded.

"The satellite readings of timespan at the foliage of both yours and Dr Zahid's wristbands shows 4.69041575982 minutes, ok? You can see the numbers I'm reading here on my laptop screen as I point it out to you..."

"Next, I see two satellite timespan readings for Kayden and then two satellite timespan readings for Kayla, look at this, it shows for Kayden's first timespan entry 1.4832399742 minutes

Second timespan entry 4.69041575982 minutes"

"Now look at Kayla's it shows the exact same just for argument's sake let's also read hers, shall we?"

"Kayla satellite readings:

First timespan entry 1.48323969742 minutes

Second timespan entry 4.69041575982 minutes."

"Whoa, but I don't get it first off how come the kids have two entries and Dr Zahid and I have only one entry on both the satellite and wristbands? Something's not right, they were with us the whole time"

"Were they?"

"What? why do you ask?"

"Think carefully Victoria, was there a point in time, a moment even small, that the kids were at a certain spot you were not aware of?'

Victoria sighed "well they did tell us that they went and collected some rocks at the foliage while we were standing at the end of the shrine pass road looking at the map on Dr. Zahid's phone."

"Ah I see, and did they say where they went? No worries, everyone's fine, I'm just showing you a discovery here please once again bear with me."

"Ok, so here's what happened, I was looking at them then at Dr Zahid for one short minute when suddenly the kids came and told us they were at the foliage, I even asked the Dr how were they able to go at the foliage and still be able to come back and tell us the story, before I even lifted my head back from looking at Dr Zahid's phone, all in the span of one minute. I didn't understand it, by I just dismissed it, when they said It, all happened while I was looking at the phone."

"Hmm do you like math?"

"Excuse me what?" Victoria asked with a small laugh as the question was so out of context.

"Umm in an average kind of way but I wasn't too bad in school either"

"Ok now take a look at this...being a mathematician, numbers speak to me like messages, they stand out, even in sequences and so forth. So let me speed track through this. Yours and Dr Zahid's minutes on the wristbands reads:

22 and the Satellite reads 4.69041575982, well guess what the square root of 22 is

$\sqrt{22} = 4.69041575982$

and now Kayden and Kayla's first timespan on their beepers shows what?

2.2 minutes, again guess what the square root of 2.2 is

$\sqrt{2.2} = 1.48323969742$, the long numbers of minutes from the satellite readings are literally the square roots of the number of minutes from your wristbands and beepers.

"Oh my God, that can't be a coincidence, how is that even possible? so what does all this means?"

"According to real-time readings from the Satellite Kayden and Kayla unknowingly experienced a Time Jump the first time they went."

"Woah, what?? I'm sorry but that's impossible."

"Please, can you do me a favor Victoria, let me explain the discovery and observation in its entirety without interruption, then once I'm done, you can comment or ask me questions, is that ok?" Simon asked while smiling, amused.

Victoria's cheeks flushed embarrassed "of course, Simon my apologies."

"no need I understand, ok so let me start over, according to real-time readings from the satellite, Kayden and Kayla unknowingly experienced a Time Jump the first time they went through the foliage, that is why what seemed to be reading 2.2 minutes on their beepers was 1.48 and so on minutes in the Satellite...that's why you asked yourself how the children went supposedly, collected rocks and came back so fast, well there was I believe also an unnatural boost, outside force speed as the time jump happened back and forth for the kids" He paused.

"And then the time jump happened a second time when all four of you went through the foliage, to you all if felt like 22 minutes, even your gadgets recorded as such, but in fact was only 4.69 and so on minutes the square root of those 22 minutes" Simon paused again allowing time for Victoria to process this giant wave of information.

He then continued on "that's also why our Satellite shows a small glitch during those specific points in time, look at the screen, during in those moments in time, your signal disappears briefly then reappears on our satellite map with those short minutes square rooted timestamps."

"And you know what else Victoria? You won't believe this but I looked into the Evangelical Brotherhood of Gold Monastery...and guess what? on their building plans and within the Brotherhood, the name of that specific location with that foliage is..."

"What's it called?" she asked completely intrigued.

"It's called Square Root Sanctuary, because the shape of the terrain at that location is a square shape and the foliage grows backward...in reverse...from the roots in the ground on one side of the wall then goes up only to fall unto the other side that's how it got its name Square Root Sanctuary."

"Wow, foliage growing backward...the number of minutes equating to their square root in the time jump...I feel like in I'm in a Sci-fi movie."

"Oh yes I'm with you, none of this can be logically explained...which drives me to my conclusion on this discovery...there is someone or a group of people with some type of an unimaginable power that gives them the ability to wield time out of their own volition and whoever this person is, they were unto all four of you at Project Exodus..."

"Now are they mal-intentioned? I'm not sure, my gut feeling tells me No but again who knows, I could be wrong."

"That is beyond surreal, I mean."

"I know, I know it sounds crazy, but I've gone over it many times, there's no other plausible explanation as it's all tracing back to the Gold Brotherhood."

"Well, that sure is a lot to take in, but thank you for your time and effort in showing me this."

"My pleasure Victoria, it was nothing, I'm passionate about puzzles and numbers, have an amazing and safe flight back home, I hope you will sign up for our next Project Exodus" Simon waved smiling, and with all his belongings packed, then he paused before leaving and said "one last thing Victoria, Dr Zahid told me, there was a man from the Gold Brotherhood you all met...he described him as, unlike anyone he's ever seen before...He said there was something superhuman about him..." Victoria's heart beat stronger than usual.

"Uh yeah, he...he was very peculiar and powerful" she didn't want to say much.

"His name is Priest Superior Clem Kedezih...he holds the supreme title in the entire brotherhood in both locations... Dr. Zahid told me he was very kind, humble even, trying to appear 'normal'" Victoria was shocked at what she heard.

"I had no idea about who he really is..."

"It's ok Victoria, somehow I just thought you should know...I have to go, glad to have worked with you, see you next time."

"Yes, thank you Simon, for everything" they both smiled and Simon left.

Victoria went back to her hotel amazed, with the strong feeling that the Gold Brotherhood is much more than what it appears to be and the mystery man of the Red Rose is right at the center of its willpower, but she still has no idea what he wants from her and does not want to find out or get any closer to the enigmatic man.

CHAPTER 9

MISSION IMPOSSIBLE

Seattle, Washington 7:30 pm

"THANKS AGAIN FOR picking me up at the airport yesterday"

Victoria said, truly grateful to have an amazing best friend.

"No worries, Hun, I know how pricey rides from the airport can be, plus always a pleasure to help, you're family" they both hugged as they sat in Victoria's living room with their favorite snacks.

"I still can't believe what you told me about Simon Peter's observation, now what are you going to do about it?"

"I'm not going to pry on what those surreal occurrences were at Project Exodus"

"Why not? Be honest with yourself..."

“Well, it’s quite simple, I don’t want to be involved in uncovering the mysteries of the Brotherhood.”

“Ah I see...in other words, you mean the mysterious man of the Rose...the Elder...” Isa-Elle said, then she added.

“You know what...? I think you’re right; you have the Rose and a Diamond sitting in your chest of drawers, we have yet to look into.”

“Exactly and by the way, this reminded me of the favor, I wanted to ask you along with what I was going to talk to you about.”

“Yes, sure you can ask away” Isa-Elle said.

“So, when you figuratively mentioned microscope, I had a great idea...we should probably bring these two mystery items at a lab, and literally study them under a microscope then_” Victoria asked

“Whoa slow down detective, are you sure about this?”

Victoria nodded yes.

“The question is how do we get into a lab, to get access to a state-of-the-Art microscope?” Victoria

“Wait a minute, you said ‘We’ as in you and I?” Isa-Elle asked suspiciously

“My dear best friend who else can I get help from than one of the most intelligent laboratory assistants I know...” Victoria paused looking at her friend with pleading eyes, and batting eyelashes.

“Yes, yes go on...” Isa-Elle replied playfully after a brief silence

“Why aren’t you saying anything?” she asked Victoria

wanting her to go on with the praises and compliments.

"Why dear, I'm just absolutely stupefied by your remarkable display of humility ...so impressive" Victoria said.

They stared at each other and laughed.

"Ok fine, let's do this, but It will have to be on my off day, which is tomorrow actually."

"Wait why your off day? Shouldn't it be on a work day? As an excuse to constantly be at the lab?"

"No, much better on my day off, where I'm not being monitored by the payroll machine If you get my meaning."

"Yeah, you're right makes sense, so we go tomorrow then?"

"No, we go tonight."

"Why? Won't it look suspicious or even dangerous?"

"Look Hun, we're not accessing a lab at the Pentagon, we're getting into the college of Experimental Science in the great University of Seattle...'

"Sorry you lost me at us going tonight, which I thought is technically your work day...Ah I see... unless we go at midnight tonight" Victoria looked at her friend with a small smile now understanding what Isa-Elle had in mind.

"Exactly at midnight, all the computers do a three-hour maintenance reboot..."

"Yess, you've told me that before, aka 3HMR"

"Correct, not everyone knows about it, in fact the only reason I know what 3HMR is, happened by accident, when the supervising research scientist I work under fell ill one day and told me to retrieve documents from the lab, I knew I didn't have the proper clearance, he told me about the 3HMR and made me sign under oath so to speak for my discretion"

"Ah that makes sense, he must trust you…ok so to recap, we Rendezvous at midnight, inside UW at the college of experimental science"

"Actually, I think it's best if we meet by the coffee shop it's next to."

"The college building, I know, sounds great."

"Awesome, allright gotta go, see you later, don't forget to bring those special items with you!" as they both walked to the door.

"Nope I won't forget that's for sure" as the door closed Victoria looked at the clock, and it was only 8:45 pm, and she realized time is definitely of the essence, they had to meet at 12 midnight sharp.

More than three and half hours later, midnight

UW Seattle-Campus.

"So here we are, finally made it" Victoria said as both friends took the elevator to the third floor of the College of the experimental science building.

"Lab room 405, two more doors and we should be there" Isa-Elle said.

"Great, 405" Victoria said as they found the door number a few minutes later.

Isa-Elle swiped her badge and the door opened.

Victoria was expecting to see a room full of scientific research papers and machinery but was surprised to see a very neat and cozy room with a small living area to her left, then to her right was a glass door, a double door but not see-through.

"Here we are, so far so good" Isa-Elle.

"This is not what I expected, the much-anticipated Lab 405 to look like."

"I know what you mean, I had the same reaction too, the first time Professor Kimble sent me here...neat and cozy for a lab."

"Yeah exactly, this could totally throw someone off if they were not very observant." Victoria replied.

"Yep definitely, ok it's the glass door, follow me" Isa-Elle said as she typed in a code the double door slid open quietly.

The Lab was bigger than she imagined, Victoria thought.

There were two large microscopes the size of computers right at the center of the room.

"Hmm interesting how the glass doors aren't see-through from the outside, only the inside..."

"Yes, pretty cool right."

"Ok let's see what this microscope will show us" Isa-Elle said.

"Wait but there's two microscopes, and they look different" Victoria replied.

"And you are right Vee, ok the one on the left is called Transmission Electron Microscope or TEM and on the right is a Scanning Electron Microscope or SEM."

“Allright Professor Isa-Elle please do tell me the difference between the two” Victoria asked with a teasing tone while Isa-Elle chuckled.

“Well, my dear, listen carefully” she responded playfully then continued on.

“TEM uses a particle beam of electrons to visualize specimens and generate a highly magnified image, those TEM types are really efficient, they can magnify objects up to 2 million times...”

“Whoa that’s like super micro micro” Victoria replied as she shook her head astonished.

“What about this one?” Victoria asked, pointing to the one on the right.

“I know right double micro for sure and yes the SEMs produce images of a sample by scanning the surface with a focused beam of electrons which then interact with atoms in the sample. That interaction then produces different signals that contain information about two things...the surface topography and the composition of the sample.”

“Sorry I know I talked a lot, so let’s not waste time and do it.”

“But how do we know which one to use in order to take a look at the items?” Victoria asked.

“Oh, I got an idea let try both items under both microscopes, I’ll take the Red Rose, you take the Diamond... we try them on each, print out the recorded data from each experiment...”

“Oh, I see, and then we switch microscopes.”

"Exactly."

"That's genius!" Victoria said, excited.

"Right! Let's do this, we're on the clock."

Victoria went under the TEM microscope and placed the diamond "oh…my…goodness gracious…what is this man?" Victoria was frozen in shock after looking into the microscope, she then lifted her head only to see that her best friend across the room had also lifted her head in absolute awe whispering "Impossible."

The two friends were now looking at each other, Isa-Elle opened her mouth to speak.

"Victoria, this is."

"Shhh don't say anything…let's not say anything to each other yet about what we saw in these microscopes or we'll run out of time" Victoria said breathing heavily like she ran a marathon; she felt her heart beating fast.

Isa-Elle nodded "ok ok you're right, let's gather all the recorded data and images we pulled from the microscopes, switch, do the same thing and get out of here before 3HMR is up, we'll talk about it in the car…" both women were startled by the sound of Isa-Elle's phone ringing.

"Oh, it's your brother, let me take this and you get going with the SEM, hey babe."

Isa-Elle answered as she walked away.

Victoria placed the diamond under the SEM, and was in complete astonishment, once again, she wiped her eyes, thinking she might not be seeing clearly and looked.

"Unbelievable" she whispered.

“Isa-Elle...” she paused because her friend had already come back after her phone call, she had placed the Red Rose under the TEM and now was looking at Victoria eyes wide, mouth slightly opened completely stupefied at what she saw.

“Ok great, found it, I’ll probably look into that tomorrow, it’s too late, gotta get back to preparing that exam...yep burning the midnight oil for sure” a man was speaking on his phone as he walked into the room and grabbed a laptop.

“Shh shh someone just walked in” Victoria told Isa-Elle, both friends quickly hid behind a set of tall vases as the double doors slightly opened.

“it’s professor Kimble...” Isa-Elle whispered.

“what’s he doing here at this time of night?” Victoria asked,

Isa-Elle looked at both herself and her friend with eyebrows raised.

“Is that a rhetorical question dear?” she said amusedly.

“He must have forgotten something...Ah yes I see it, it’s his laptop” Victoria whispered in reply

“Ok brother, see you tomorrow at the luncheon.”

Professor Kimble said as he stepped out of the lab, then... he suddenly slows down and turns to look around the lab for a moment, then turned off the lights and walked out, all the while, both women were holding their breath, Victoria was certain professor Kimble must have seen them.

They exhaled in relief as they heard the professor exit the room and heard his firm steps retreating down the hallway.

"Oh my God, I thought it was over for us..." Victoria said in relief, breathing fast.

"let's get out of here before we get any more surprise visitors" Isa-Elle as they quickly left the room.

Thirty minutes later...

"Let's talk tomorrow, my place around lunchtime?" Victoria asked Isa-Elle on the phone as she sat on her bed.

"Oh, actually I can't around lunchtime give me an hour... in the afternoon would that work? Like one pm-ish?"

"Yeah, sounds great, see you then..."

"Goodnight, Hun."

"goodnight" Victoria replied.

CHAPTER 10

SPARKS

THE NEXT DAY at Victoria's place 1:30 pm, Isa-Elle had just walked in, the women sat in the dining room:

"I barely slept" Victoria said.

"Me too, same here."

"Ok you go first, what did you see in the microscope?"

"Victoria...there were small specks of genuine gold all over the rose" she paused then continued on

"And then I moved the lens focus toward the stem when I saw it..." she paused again.

"Saw what? you're kind of scaring me with your pauses."

"I'm not trying to scare you, actually this is nothing to be scared about...honestly it's all so surreal, beautiful but intimidating at the same time."

"Thank you for the reassurance sis, now tell me what you saw...please" Both women looked at each other briefly in silence.

"The Stem had a message on it written for you, in fact it's carved in pure Gold, but somehow invisible to the naked eye, it can only be read under a sophisticated microscope."

"What does the message say?"

"Here, this is a printout of the Gold specks image and this is the message...I think you should read it yourself" Isa-Elle handed her both documents.

"Okay...Thanks, alright let's see."

'And when I passed by again, I saw that you were old enough for love. So, I wrapped my cloak around you to cover your nakedness, and declared my marriage vows. I made a covenant with you, says the sovereign LORD, and you became mine."

She gasped.

"I...I don't understand any of it" Victoria was in shock.

"I myself have no idea dear, but before we go any further, what did you see inside the diamond?"

"I saw...nothing."

"What? wait what do you mean you saw nothing."

"I mean I saw something that I thought was nothing but then realized it might be something" Victoria said

"Wow, first and foremost I had no Idea you could talk that fast" they both laughed.

"Soo what's that something you saw?"

"I, I don't know how to even describe it, they were multiples, strange patterns within the structure of the diamond, I mean I have never seen anything like it...what are you doing?" as Victoria was talking, she noticed that her friend quickly grabbed her phone and was attentively reading from it.

"As you were talking, I just got an idea, like a major one, but before I tell you, listen to this, you'll get what I mean, so I'll be reading for a minute, just listen ok?" Isa-Elle said as Victoria nodded.

"Ok here goes, this article says that as the light moves through a diamond it is scattered and fractured...this is the refraction...this refraction and dispersion also creates natural light and dark areas in the refracted light, depending on where the light hits along the planes of the diamond..."

"So, what you mean is like a reflection..."

"Hang on darling, wait I'm almost done, you gotta listen to this, here it says 'these facets, along with how the diamond effects wavelengths of light' watch this...

'Disperses it into a rainbow' of colors like light through a prism..." she paused.

"This creates the flashes of color called 'Fire'"

"Ok...so what you're saying is, we can try and shine light through the diamond?" Victoria asked completely intrigued as this could work, she thought.

"Yess, that's exactly what I mean, then maybe we'll get a message from those patterns..." suddenly the doorbell rang,

"Hold that thought" Victoria said as she walked over to the door, looked through the peephole then froze, eyes wide she took a step back "Hmph" Victoria bumped into her friend as she also seeing Victoria's strange reaction, quickly walked to check if she was ok.

"What? what is it Victoria, who's at the door?"

"It's Dr. Zahid Hassan, the physicist teacher I told you about from Project Exodus…how did he get my address and why is he here, that's a little creepy."

"Ok Hun, first off you need to calm down…I'm your bodyguard, I know a thing or two about Karate."

Isa-Elle said with an amused expression on her face,

"Oh, is that so?" Victoria said laughing, as she felt peace, and at that moment she was even more thankful that her best friend was here with her, as so many strange events have been taking place around her, there was a firm knock on the door, that startled both women, Victoria decided all these questions might be answered by Dr Zahid who knows, she thought then finally opened the door.

"Miss Victoria, first I would like to truly apologize for this impromptu visit…" He seemed embarrassed as he handed her a bouquet of flowers.

"These are a variety of flowers species I had picked from the Gold Monastery's secret garden we visited on Project Exodus."

"Um Dr. Zahid thank you for the apology and the flowers, but it is absolutely impertinent and even uncivil of you to retrieve my personal address without my consent and furthermore pay me a visit…"

"That is exactly why I apologize and the flowers are

simply a token to express my regrets, it was my wife and granddaughter's idea."

Victoria's heart softened as she heard the mention of his wife and granddaughter, she felt comforted by it somehow and decided to let him inside.

"Thank you, Dr. Zahid, I accept your apology, please come in, this is my best friend and sister-in-law Isa-Elle" they shook hands.

Victoria brought both guests to her living room.

"Can I get you anything to drink Dr?"

"No, I'm ok thank you..."

"You traveled all the way here, let me get you least some... sparkling water, would that work?" Victoria asked feeling remorseful for the way she overreacted at the door.

Her best friend smiled at her reassuringly, understanding exactly what was going through her mind."

"Yes, sparkling water works fine, thank you" Dr. Zahid smiled and added as he looked around.

"I must say, this is a nice place you have here"

"Thank you and here you go" Victoria replied as she brought the drinks for all three of them and sat down.

"Ok I won't be too long, but considering the importance of the discovery I made, the past couple of days, I had to see you in person."

"Sure Dr, I understand, please go on."

"That day, the children Kayden and Kayla from Project Exodus came back with stones as we were standing on the shrine pass, you remember that right?"

"Yes, I do, I remember the details of that particular day very well"

"Ok good, now the two precious stones we saw inside those rocks, I took them to my office after Project Exodus, to study them and then breakdown their composition to verify their authenticity." He shook his head in amazement.

"What did you find?"

"I was unable to identify any of its properties, it didn't correspond to any of our chemical elements on the periodic table"

"What does it mean when it's not on the periodic table?" Isa-Elle asked.

"It concludes that the stones do not originate from our world" there was complete silence.

Victoria and Isa-Elle looked at each other, then back at Dr. Zahid.

"Miss Victoria...you didn't look so surprised, neither do you" he pointed at Isa-Elle.

"Do you know something I don't?"

"Please call me Victoria, the answer to your question is yes, but before I explain further, I'm curious as to why you're telling me this...shouldn't you be informing your science team, your colleagues, superiors, or even the National Science foundation...?"

"Yes, you're absolutely right, but somehow my guts tells me that, it wouldn't be the way to go, because you see, I am quite observant and I took my time at Project Exodus..."

"What do you mean?'

"The stones were given to the children by Elder Clem who is, in fact, the Priest Superior of the entire monastery cloister, I came all the way from Colorado because I noticed his interaction with you Victoria...it was unlike anything I've seen, I'm not quite sure how to explain this but he gave me the impression of being more than just a man."

"What do you mean by more than a man?" Isa-Elle asked.

"The Priest Superior is not ordinary, he is extraordinary, I would dare to say superhuman and you miss Victoria...I mean Victoria; you have somehow caught his attention in a very possessive and passionate way..." Dr. Zahid said.

Then he continued on; all the while Victoria was quiet, amazed because she has for the first time heard an observation of the mysterious man of the rose from a point of view other than her own...Dr. Zahid is the first-ever witness to the man of the Rose's unusual interest,

"The way he was looking at you Victoria, was more than just ordinary human interest, at some point his eyes seem to emit some type of luminosity? I thought certainly I must have imagined it, but no, I know what I saw...I mean it's so strange, and these rocks came from him, so I felt it would be more effective to talk to you about my discoveries, plus we were both there at Project Exodus, I figured why not tell you instead"

"Oh...my God" Victoria whispered.

"Did you see that too?" Dr. Zahid said.

"I'm sorry see what?"

"His eyes...how they were such an intense burnt orange/brown, so fiery..."

"No, I didn't..." Victoria whispered.

"We made a discovery ourselves..."

"Isa-Elle! What are you doing?" Victoria said.

"You can trust me Victoria, I flew over here to share this information with you because I feel you can be trusted."

"Yes, I do feel that too about him Vee," Victoria looked at her friend for a moment.

"He gave you something didn't he?" Dr. Zahid said.

"Yes, he did, a rose and a rock."

"Did the rock or the rose have anything strange on them?" Dr. Zahid said.

"Yes...the rose had a hidden message..."

"What was the message?"

"I'd rather not say just yet, I'm sorry I'm trying to figure all this out, all I can say is; it was very...intimate."

"Hmm, no worries I understand, this is so unusual."

"Yes very..."

"What about the rock, anything?"

"Thinking of what happened with the children's rocks back at Exodus, I decided to try and crack the rock, and um a diamond was inside."

"Unbelievable..." Dr. Zahid whispered.

Victoria then proceeded in telling Dr. Zahid about their microscopes' discoveries.

"If we tried and shine a light through the diamond, would it show us a legible pattern you think?" Isa-Elle said.

"May I see it?" Dr. Zahid said.

"Yes, one second" Victoria handed over the diamond to him, Dr. Zahid pulled a magnifying glass out and placed it over the diamond.

"Hmm...in all my 30 years of experience, I've never seen anything like it...simply extraordinary"

"You saw something else on it?" Victoria said.

"There is a minuscule deposit of gold specks sitting at the bottom."

"Whoa, how come I didn't see it under a microscope?" Victoria said.

"Incredible" Isa-Elle whispered.

"I'm not sure, maybe this particular diamond has different facets that you would see strictly under a magnifying glass" Dr. Zahid said.

"What do you suggest?" Victoria asked.

There was silence as Dr. Zahid stared intensely at the diamond.

Victoria was breathing deeper than usual,

"We're not alone" she whispered.

"Goodness gracious! What was that? Did you see that flash of light Vee?"

"The diamond" Dr. Zahid said.

"Feels like it winked at us" Isa-Elle said.

"Yes, something happened, strange..." Dr. Zahid said,

then he asked.

"Victoria? Are you ok?"

Victoria also saw the diamond odd flash of light ricochet from the wall back to itself,

"Yes it 'winked' as you call it" she was breathing normally again.

"Quantum Teleportation" Dr. Zahid said still looking into the diamond almost in a transient state.

"Sorry the what now?" Isa-Elle said.

"Dr. Zahid what's that?" Victoria said.

"The diamond, the message stored inside was done through Quantum Teleportation"

"What makes you say that? And what is it exactly?" Victoria said.

"Hun, I have to go, call me when you're free, and it was nice meeting you Dr. Zahid" Isa-Elle said as she stood with Victoria walking to the door.

"Likewise, Isa-Elle, take care" Dr. Zahid replied absentmindedly.

she smiled, the best friends hugged and the door closed.

Victoria was now back on the couch.

"After the diamond 'winked' so to speak, something strange happened not quite sure how to explain it but" Dr. Zahid said.

"Wait Dr you were about to explain how Quantum Teleportation"

"I'm getting to that Victoria, patience" He smiled kindly

with a fatherly reprimanding look.

Victoria could feel the heat on her flushed cheeks as she realized the need to work on her habit of interrupting in mid conversations.

"As I was saying after the diamond 'winked', my mind became very clear, and I knew right away in what way the message in the diamond was hidden...two words popped into my mind crystal clear 'Quantum Teleportation'"

"Oh my God..."

"From what I know, it's still a novelty but basically it all started in Japan" He paused drank his water and continued on.

"A team of researchers from the Yokohama National University in Japan did something that's never been done before" Victoria could hear the padded sound of Dr. Zahid's feet as he began pacing back and forth across the room.

"Wow, amazing."

"They have managed to teleport quantum information securely into one of the hardest structures on earth, guess what that is?"

"The diamond?"

"Yes, the diamond and there's a lot involved in the process, I mean from photons carrying the quantum information to magnetic field creation, usage of microwaves and radio to entangle the electron and the carbon atom's nucleus."

"Dr. Zahid? Dr. thank you but my non-scientific brain

can only take so much" Victoria said chuckling

"My apologies, I got a little carried away in my physicist's world" he said smiling

"Dr. I want to know what message is stored in that diamond, what will it take to retrieve the quantum information? will you please help me?" she said.

Dr. Zahid sighed as he was getting ready to leave "Victoria I will do my best and hope we succeed."

"Thank you Dr. I'm truly grateful" she said while walking Dr. Zahid to the door, as it closed, Victoria went back into the living room, grabbed her bible and laptop along with the microscopes' transcripts, set them all on the table. Looking up the wording inscribed on the Rose.

"Ezekiel 16:8...why me?" Victoria was baffled by all the strange occurrences, she placed her bible on the table closed it, and laid back on her couch.

"He's so...disturbingly intimate" she said aloud frowning, his physical temperament was very foreign to her, very vibrant, like a magnet.

Victoria's vision blurred slightly, feeling sleepy.

"I guess a nap wouldn't hurt" yawning, Victoria felt the soft cotton fabric of her living room pillow as she laid down on the couch, all was quiet, Bandjo had an extended vacation at her sister's.

Her eyes were blinking slowly, her gaze became dimmer until suddenly.

"Oh my God!" Victoria had felt something touch her lips and jumped off the couch, fully alert, her heart beating strongly, she had... Rose petals all over her from head to toe and on the floor

"What in the world..." Victoria whispered, as she sat on the couch again with multiple red rose petals around her, she noticed that...red petals went all the way down to where she sat, forming a specific trail then went back up to the table and laid on the open bible, which she was certain was closed before taking her nap, she took a picture then decided to count the red rose petals on the couch and the ones on the opened bible.

She counted 16 red rose petals on the couch, including the one that landed on her lips.

she asked herself "I felt a petal on my lips earlier? Or was it something else..." she counted 8 red rose petals on her opened bible.

"I've never seen anything like this."

She looked at the verse, her bible was opened to Ezekiel 16:8,

"What in the world...the rose petals landed exactly on Ezekiel 16:8, 16 petals on the couch, 8 petals on the Bible."

Victoria sat up straight on the couch, suddenly she realized, she wasn't alone.

"He's here..." she whispered, her heart beating faster than normal.

CHAPTER 11

OUT OF THE BLUE

Somewhere near Vail Mountain,
Eagle County,
Colorado.

"WELL, SO FAR this is not what I expected" Gabe Sinatra told one of the tour guides as he and seven other tourists were walking up a trail in the mountains.

"What were you expecting?" a tour guide named Jesse asked him.

"Much more than just two hours of national geographic on TV about mountain climbing and little outside exploration"

"Oh, I understand, unfortunately, that's how they have these touristic events set up" she replied.

"All right It's like noon right now, so what's the plan? I

know they explained it to us for 2 hours in that meeting room...but please I just need the short version."

He said humorously, Jesse chuckled.

"Ok...Here's the plan" she replied, and then paused noticing that the entire team had stopped in their tracks and came around to listen to the plan being laid out.

"Okay...is that everyone?" Jesse asked.

"Yep, all eight tourists and two tour guides" a woman in the group replied

"Thanks, all right" Jesse pulled out a paper and would briefly look at it for reference.

"From Eagle Vail, where we are now, we will pass through Vail Mountain on our left. Then we head up Tigiwon road to the start of the trail..."

"Excuse me, when you say 'we will head up...and pass through, you mean by car right?" A man asked her

"Correct by car, we wouldn't be able to cover that much ground on foot, any other questions?"

When no one spoke up, she then continued on.

"Ok, so our goal is to either get to the summit of Holy Cross mount for those ambitious enough or close to it for those who would still be satisfied without having reached the summit. Alright now let's get moving and also explore as you go, I always say 'sure the summit is great, but it's also the journey to the summit that makes this whole experience worth it...ok enough talking from me; let's have an adventure" she smiled as some whistles sounded.

"Nice speech there" Gabe said as they were walking.

"Thanks, after ten years in the hospitality industry, you learn a few things...those words are actually what my husband says often."

"You both must be passionate about this" Gabe said.

"Yes, we started our own small venture a few years ago in the travel and touristic arena and here we are, landed a contract with a big travel company interested in what we do, it's been a blessing for our whole family since."

"Well, you're really good at it, I'm happy for you and your family, you kind of remind me of my mom, but in a younger version if I may say."

"Thanks! I take that as a compliment" Jesse said.

"Yes, mom is high on hospitality, so precise, everything has to be neat and at the same time, she loves adventures, discoveries, like a child"

"Funny enough to say but that's me!" she said laughing

Gabe laughed at her reaction.

"I thought so..." whoosh!

"Hey! Guys! Did y'all hear that?" another tourist asked

"What was that?" Gabe asked Jesse as they were all heading to their cars to make the short drive as planned, the team was five miles closer to the shrine pass.

"What are you all doing here?" a sheriff asked as he walked up to them with another man in tow, the other man was wearing civilian clothes, very authoritative and a bit of an arrogant air in his bold countenance and audacious eyes.

"FBI?" Jesse whispered referring to the man walking

along with the Sheriff.

"No, or maybe, I'm not sure, he might be something else" Gabe replied as he kept looking at the man with the brown jacket and blue jeans.

"who's in charge here?" the sheriff asked.

Whoosh! Again, the sound echoed against the nearby mountain walls, right after the sheriff asked his question, as if to add more emphasis.

All eyes turned toward Gabe, startled, He stepped back then realized the team's look was directed at Jesse who stood next to him.

"I am" Jesse said raising her hand.

Gabe couldn't shake out his curiosity about the identity of the man in brown and blue, especially since the man was now staring at him.

"May I speak with you briefly, in private mam" the Sheriff asked Jesse, as she, the officer, and the man stepped aside.

Jesse was nodding slowly as the officer spoke, the other man was following the conversation with both hands behind his back, he looked at Gabe, their gaze met, which was strange considering he was now standing among the other tourists.

"Who is this guy?" Gabe asked no one in particular.

"I know right, he's kinda weird, not really but just weird in a normal way...you know what I'm sayin?"

A young man about 18 years old replied to Gabe's question.

"Right" Gabe said amused.

"Ok you all, I'm sorry to say this but this area and the one leading to Holy Cross mount has been declared by the mayor, a restricted area" Jesse said as she joined the group.

"Oh, come on! That's not fair" one person said.

"What? I don't' understand, did they say why?" then another voice sounded until the whole team was speaking over each other.

"Hey guys, listen we still have alternatives, there are various locations, the monastery, the Glory Dome, Vail Mountain, we can still hike through part of the trail..." Jesse kept speaking, but her voice faded away in Gabe's ears, as his focus was on the sheriff and the man he came along with.

He seemed to be ranking higher than the officer, he was giving him instructions, the man lifted his right hand, pointing at an area before them...

"Whoa, what's that?" Gabe said, he saw something on the man's right hand.

"A tattoo?" he thought.

It was a blue marking, on the man's hand close to the base of his outer wrist, it was clear enough to see from a distance because of the marking's unusual iridescence, this strange mark was luminous, lighting up a vibrant blue.

"What is he? Secret service? Special forces? The NSA?" he thought.

"Gabe? Gabe" Jesse called out.

"Sorry, I was gone for a while" he said.

"I can understand why, that guy's strange, and looks like

he's the one calling the shots"

"Have you seen him before?"

"No, never seen him in my whole five years of working here."

"Hmm, strange" Gabe said as he kept looking at the black SUV where the man got in, now driving away with the Sheriff's car in front of him.

"We're splitting up in two groups, there's been a vote, to choose between the monastery or hiking through part of the trail to explore"

"Ok got it" Gabe said.

"All right that's great but what do you pick?" Jesse said then asked

"Gabe are you ok?"

"Yeah, I'm fine sorry, I just..."

"Ok if you say so, because you look very distracted my friend."

"No, I'm ok really, I choose hiking the trail."

"Allright, the trail hike is scheduled for tomorrow."

"Wait, why tomorrow? Why not today?"

"Since we don't have time to accommodate both locations for tourists in today, we had split the group in half and do two days instead of one, the Brotherhood had extended the touristic event to two days this year, which is a surprise."

"Why?"

"I see now, you're very inquisitive," Jesse said chuckling.

Gabe shrugged "that's why I started with an English

major and ended up in the science field."

"Yep, now I know why, well the Brotherhood always and I mean always year after year since the 1940's does One day only touristic event."

"There must be something special this time around."

"Hmm" Jesse replied.

"Well see you tomorrow."

"I won't be there tomorrow; it'll be either my husband or my oldest son."

"Ah gotcha, well it was nice meeting you, and thank you for sorting this out, more like improvising."

"Oh yes, you do what you have to, always a pleasure" Jesse started walking away.

"One more thing," Gabe said.

"Yes," she said turning around.

"What were those loud sounds we heard earlier? Before the man and the sheriff came and also while y'all were talking, it sounded again," Gabe asked.

"Oh, those sounds, I honestly have no clue," Jesse said.

"And Gabe, you also remind me of someone, my little brother."

"Oh really? How?"

"His avid awareness of his surroundings, his fearless curiosity, to figure out hidden mysteries"

"Thank you, I'll take that as a compliment as well."

"Sure, but one piece of advice I always give him...well two pieces of advice, one is to be careful with this search of the unknown and unexplainable, to take it at face value and everything is not always some fantastic adventure as it could have consequences affecting him for life.

"Yes, thank you, I feel this advice is for me too, isn't it?" Jesse didn't respond and just looked at him smiling.

"So, what's the other advice? You said two."

"To get married and have kids."

"See that's where he and I are different, I am in fact getting married" Gabe chuckled.

"Oh, that's amazing, congratulations. Well, it was a pleasure meeting you Gabe, take care of yourself."

"You as well and I will" He looked at his watch as Jesse walked away.

Gabe decided to look further into the blue symbol on the man's wrist as he returned to the extended stay hotel he booked in Redcliff.

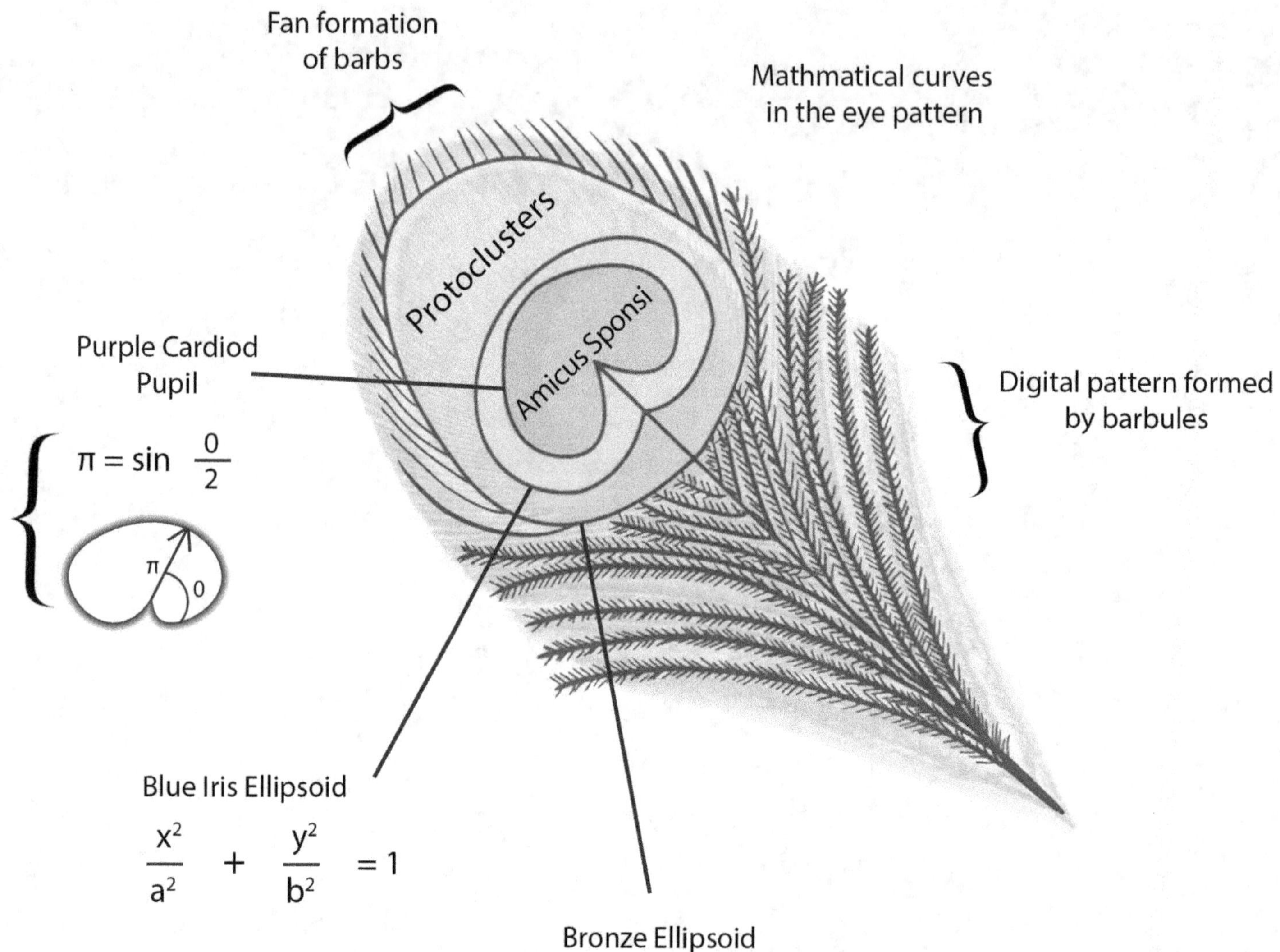
Fan formation
of barbs
Mathmatical curves
in the eye pattern
Protoclusters
Amicus Sponsi
Purple Cardiod
Pupil
Digital pattern formed
by barbules
π = sin 0/2
π
0
Blue Iris Ellipsoid
x²/a² + y²/b² = 1
Bronze Ellipsoid

CHAPTER 12

A DETOUR

Day Two

"BRO, A BLUE peacock's feather?"

"Yes, now that I think about it, this is what his tattoo looked like, do you think it means anything?"

"Hmm, not sure, considering the way you described him, it might or it might not"

"How soon can you find out?"

"Little brother, don't get too caught up with this strange guy's identity..."

"Please Houston, I really need your help...I must find out who that is"

He could hear Houston sigh over the phone.

"Ok...I'll help you."

"Thank you so much..." Gabe said.

"Hold on, I'm not done, I'll help you, in one condition."

"Please let it not be, letting mom and Dad in on this, or even Zena, just for now, let's keep this between us."

"Are you done?" Houston asked chuckling even though, Gabe was the youngest, making both brother's age difference quite significant, a thirteen years gap to be exact, Houston and Gabe were extremely close, like best friends.

Gabe would often remember so many adventures they had growing up, including the fights and troubles they got into.

"My bad, go ahead" Gabe said.

"Allright, my one condition is that you tell me everything that goes on, I mean every detail, capiche?"

"Ok cool, but bro sometimes you kinda creep me out."

"What do you mean?"

"You sound like Pops sometimes; I mean to the point where I almost said 'ok Dad'" Gabe said teasingly.

"Whatever you say, all right little ranger, gotta go, be good" Houston said the last words with their dad's voice, laughing.

"Ok stop you're milking it bro, that's just brutal" Gabe said as they all knew how Noah Sinatra always called him 'little ranger' when they were younger and still does today.

He hung up on his brother still laughing, then he realized Houston forgot to give him an ETA on when he would get back to him about the tattoo.

But he ran out of time to call back as today was Day Two for Group II going hiking on the trail.

Gabe met with Jesse's son Brian, a twenty-three-year-old college student, helping his parents on his hiatus.

They were now three miles into the trail, hiking when Gabe suddenly sees a structure he hadn't seen before on the side of the trail.

"I think I'll cut my trip short, and camp out here to take some pictures, is that ok?"

"Ah, sure no problem, I see you like the Pilgrim's hut, cool huh?" Brian said.

"Yes, it sure is, y'all can keep going, you'll find me here on your way back."

"Gabe?" He heard his name being called behind him and turned around.

"Remember that guy form yesterday?" it was the eighteen-year-old looking boy who commented on the strange man's appearance yesterday.

"Hey what's up? You allright?"

"Yeah, I'm ok" He responded.

"aren't you going with the others? I mean I don't mind the company but I'd rather work solo on this one here"

"No, you're good, I'll catch up with the others just wanted to let you know I took a pic..."

"a pic of what?"

"I took a pic of the guy from yesterday," Gabe froze, his curiosity picked.

"Really? And sorry I didn't catch your name."

"Cuz I never told you it, name's Steve."

"Ok Steve, show me the picture."

"Huh huh" Steve stared at him with a calculated look, Gabe realized what he wanted.

"So, what's it gonna take…for me to look and even get a copy of this picture?"

"Fifty bucks"

"What?? fifty b_, thirty,"

"Forty_"

"thirty-five bucks and that's final."

"Deal," Steve said smiling.

"Unbelievable" Gabe shook his head reaching for the cash, as Steve opened his phone camera roll and showed him the picture.

"Whoa, this is high quality, you got talent kid," Gabe said as he whistled in admiration, then Gabe focused on the picture and saw the man's tattoo in clear view, it wasn't just a blue Peacock's feather…there was something else.

"Ahem," Steve extended his hand.

"Oh, my bad, first off send me the pic, here's my number 333-1895."

"What's the area code?"

"281" Gabe heard a chime sound and looked at the text message, he received the picture as agreed and paid the boy.

"Seriously kid, you got talent," Gabe said.

"I'm not a kid, what's it to you anyways, see ya" Steve said as he jogged over the trail to catch up with the group.

"Kids," Gabe shook his head.

Arms akimbo, he turned, now facing the structure that caught his attention, he began walking toward it, his phone rang.

"Hey bro, I got your text that picture's high quality where'd you get it?"

"Some kid Steve, who's also on this tour, I guess he's very observant, he saw how curious I was and let's just say he decided to use his talent for profit."

"Interesting, so I zoomed in on his hand, Steve had already done a great job, the symbol is in fact a peacock's feather but when you look closer, I mean it took me a moment just staring at the pic to see it."

"See what?" Gabe asked as he finally reached the Pilgrim's Hut, standing about three feet from the stone-built structure.

"there's something in the eye of the feather, an image that you might know more about than me"

"I don't understand."

"Just zoom in on the eye of the feather and really, I mean really look at it."

"Ok...now I'm very intrigued, I'm at the pilgrim's hut right now give me a sec to get in."

"Allright...so how is it inside?"

"Well like something from the 1920s, very remarkable, what the pilgrims did" Gabe pulled up a small wooden chair.

"Ok, now I'm ready, let's see" He added, then a minute passed.

"Gabe you there?" Houston asked.

"Unbelievable bro you know what this is?"

"Not quite, I kinda figured you would."

"Protoclusters, or more like one of them, I wrote a dissertation on it in my last year of college, one example of it was, the abnormal phenomenon of fourteen separate galaxies 12.4 billion light-years away, that was showing a synchronized behavior which couldn't be explained by their individual gravitational fields."

"Ok great, now can you speak in English and explain it to me again?" Gabe chuckled.

"Allright sorry, the tattoo on this man's hand consists of a blue peacock feather, right? and within the eye of that feather there is an image of the great discovery made over the years as it began to occur in 2018, the discoveries were made by astronomers and astrophysicists, that of hundreds of galaxies rotating in sync with the motions of galaxies that were tens of millions of light-years away from each other."

"Ok, so it's not something that's common, is that what you're saying?"

"Try impossible, in space science principles it is impossible for galaxies separated by megaparsecs to directly interact with each other, I mean can you imagine? Their interaction happens across distances that are too large to be explained by their gravitational force, it's a very unusual sentient behavior and you know what they concluded? Or scratch that, rather what they speculated?"

"What?"

"These brilliant scientists deduced that some Unacknowledged Force must be acting."

"Wow, incredible."

"The question is why and how would it then end up inside some random tattoo?"

"Unless it's not random... so far Gabe, I don't know what to make of the man, we need to find out what the peacock feather means as well, but yes you're right...peacock feather with Protoclusters is a very strange choice for a tattoo."

"Yes totally, if you can do some digging on it, I'll truly appreciate it bro, and I'll do the same."

"All right, will do, gotta go, dinner time with Diana and the kids."

"Please give Diana and the troublemakers my love."

"I sure will, one more thing Gabe?"

"Yeah?"

"Be very careful, I have a feeling you're entering some uncharted waters if you get my meaning"

"Yeah, no worries I'll be fine."

"Ok I'll talk to you_"

"Shh hang on."

"What? what's wrong?"

"Keep quiet, please...I'm hearing something," He whispered.

"You taking pictures?" Houston whispered.

"Already did, but there's a sound...let me call you back."

"Ok keep me posted, be careful," Gabe hung up then he stood and walked cautiously toward the source of the sound, further into the hut.

"Strange, it's the same whoosh sound we heard yesterday."

"Hello?" Gabe noticed an entrance...a back door further into the Hut.

"Whoa, how come I didn't see this when I came in" he thought and he took pictures of the entire hut, the items of furniture and all other items, then he opened the door, expecting to see the other side of the mountain when suddenly he sees a well-lit hallway, more like a corridor with modern lighting, very neat passage with stone walls on either side.

"This is not the pilgrims' hut, it's something else," Gabe recorded himself as he lost signal when entering the corridor, he kept walking, until he reached a hallway opening in the opposite direction from the corridor he was in, forming a T shape.

"Hmm two doors," Gabe whispered, one double door on the left and a large dome-shaped double door to his right, he could hear voices chanting in peaceful harmony.

"Gregorian chant? This must be a monastery, but why in the mountains?" Gabe came closer and peeked in through the glass part of the door "a library" Gabe saw one of the most spectacular libraries he's ever seen as he peeked through the door, he could see the tall shelves filled with books and men in matching gold and brown robes walking, a small group chanting from a hymn pamphlet stood near a globe, Gabe was aware that he was witnessing a hidden historical site, listening to one of the most beautiful melodies he's ever heard.

"The monastery of the Gold Brotherhood," he whispered.

"Wow amazing."

As he kept looking through the library door something familiar caught his attention "wait a minute this is the same blue peacock feather...and the protoclusters of galaxies..."

Gabe spoke into his phone recorder "the tattoo on the man's hand from yesterday it's...some type of symbol, an emblem-it's incredible I..." Whoosh!

"Ubi Caritas" a male voice sounded from behind him startled Gabe turned around.

"What...sorry I, I don't speak Latin...it's you..."

The man nodded toward the library, somehow Gabe knew he was referring to the Latin hymn being sung by the brothers, he recognized him immediately as the man from yesterday with the strange tattoo.

"You know one thing Gabe Sinatra; trespassing is a serious crime...not only that but voice recording illegally in that premise only adds to the offense list."

"I'm sorry, who are you? How do you know my name? I don't want any trouble..."

"Hmm somehow I doubt it, that curiosity of yours will get you in very strange places...like today for example"

"My apologies for trespassing, it happened by accident."

"You being here is no accident, haven't you asked yourself, why was it so easy for you to get into our property with no obstacles? Now hand me your phone," the man said.

Gabe was shocked as he realized that he did in fact make his way here very easily... 'too easy' he thought.

"Ok look, what do you mean, this is a bit strange once again, my sincere apologies for trespassing, but I can't hand you my phone."

"The voice recording must be deleted. Even for your own safety with you being involved in this now."

"Whoa hold on a minute, I'm not involved in any of this, now I'd really be grateful if you don't press any charges, but I also can't delete this recording."

The man stopped pacing suddenly, he looked up, closed his eyes as if in prayer then reopened them, he then faced Gabe and began walking toward him.

"Hmph! wha-what's happening? Can't breathe..."

As the man got closer, Gabe fell to the ground, he felt as if a two-ton brick sat on his chest, he couldn't get up.

Suddenly two other men, he never knew were there, stepped in next to the stranger all in brown robes and gold sash, he heard the stranger say to both men as they all stood over Gabe.

"Amicus Sponsi" then the other men nodded, Gabe didn't understand what it meant, but he had a strange feeling those words were referring to him.

"I gotta get out of here, Houston, I need to call..." he thought.

He sighed with relief as the weight lifted off his chest, but he was still on the floor unable to stand, his back against the wall, his gaze went from the stranger to the second man as they were talking then he noticed something strange happening.

"What in the world..." Gabe said in amazement as the third man pulled out a pen, out of thin air and began writing on the opposite wall in superhuman speed, he wrote the words "Amicus Sponsi" and drew the emblem of the peacock, the stranger from yesterday paused in his sentence, then he looked at Gabe, suddenly the tattoo on his hand started to luminesce like it did the day before, it became so bright, Gabe lifted his arm while squinting his eyes to the blinding light...he couldn't see.

CHAPTER 13

ASCENSION

"GABE? GABE WAKE up!"

He abruptly opened his eyes, becoming aware of his surroundings.

"Houston? What are you doing here? Where are we?"

"Gabe, we're back at your hotel, I kept knocking but you weren't answering, I had the shift manager open the door."

"Here gets some water."

"Houston I_"

"Hang on, let me call downstairs and tell them we don't need an ambulance."

The entire day's event suddenly came back to Gabe as he laid on the bed.

"Allright done, so what happened?"

"Wait why are you here?"

"You mean in this hotel?"

"No why are you here in Red Cliff instead of Houston, Houston?" Gabe asked.

"Really bro? I see you feeling better now."

"Much better thanks..." Gabe said.

"And you just had to go there huh? Double H me with my own name," Gabe tried hard not to laugh as Houston shook his head.

"When we spoke last night and you heard some strange sound, then hung up quickly, immediately I started going through a tug of war in my mind, whether to come over or not."

"And you felt I needed your help..." Gabe said.

"Yes, but not just that, Diana was convinced that you were in trouble, and couldn't shake off that feeling"

"I appreciate you coming..."

"And I made a discovery" there was a pause.

"About the emblem?" Gabe said.

"Yes, and much more" Houston said.

"I can't thank you enough, what I've seen today is extraordinary."

"Hmm, before we go into that, Gabe do you remember how you made it back to the hotel?"

"Huh that's the thing, I remember everything that happened today except how I got back here, there was this blinding light and then I saw the ceiling...clouds...I don't."

"Whoa slow down bro, all right let's start from the beginning."

"What did the front desk tell you?" Gabe said.

"When I spoke with the manager, she told me on one saw you coming in"

"Strange" Gabe said.

"What's strange?"

"Is the receptionist still drinking coffee from that green foam cup she had a bad experience with?"

"Bro, you're asking the strangest question..."

"Please Houston stay with me, I'm going somewhere with this"

"Ok, no, in fact when I walked in, she said hi, then she started telling me right away how just ten minutes ago she had a bad experience with...wait a minute how did you know what she said? Her exact words, you weren't there."

"I was...but from a different vantage point, it's coming back to me a little, I could see the top of everything..."

"You mean...from bird's eye view...oh my God Gabe, what did you get yourself into..."

"I'm still trying to figure this out bro."

"Allright tell me everything."

"Ok."

Eight minutes later...

"Incredible, just surreal "Houston said after Gabe told him of his experience at the Pilgrim's hut.

"So, what did you find?"

"The feather and galaxy protocluster are the symbol of an Ancient Secret Order, that started about 80-90 AD at the time of the Apostles of Christ, I don't know their exact name, but they have a total of 777 functions..."

"Whoa, that's a lot of functions, this can't be real..."

"Oh yes, it is..."

"Were you able to get some details on some of their functions?"

"Only one, unfortunately, This Ancient Order is unlike anything I've seen or heard of in history, all I could see is just one function out of the 777... one function is to retrieve and protect pieces of information and also particular people... they weren't precise on what exactly does 'particular people' mean."

"Wow, unbelievable, even now my head is spinning because there's so much that I saw, that I can never unsee, but still, I don't understand what's happening to myself, I just know I have to find out."

Gabe stood and walked over to the window, as Houston took a seat on the couch, legs folded, he was looking out onto the hotel parking lot.

"There was this one thing from what I told you earlier, the guy with the tattoo said it to the other two guys, and by the way, I noticed that even though they were all wearing brown robes with the Gold Sash, that man was the only one with the tattoo, I just find that interesting."

"Yes, I wonder why" Houston said.

"But anyways so as the guy with the tattoo came close to

me, the other men literally appeared on either side of him, he told them some Latin words, I couldn't hear it at first because I was working hard trying to catch my breath, then I see one of the two guys pulls out a pen…out of thin air and writes on the wall across from me those same words…"

"What were the words?"

Gabe still standing by the window, looked at his brother, grateful for his loyalty and support.

"So? What were they?"

"It reads AMICUS SPONSI."

"Hang on, I just looked it up, it means Fri_ woah Gabe! Bro! what's that on your arm?!"

Gabe had lifted his right hand to scratch his neck when suddenly, there was a blue luminescent mark on his arm. Houston stood and took two big steps, held his little brother's arm for inspection.

"What in the world…" Houston said.

"Oh my God…this can't be real…" Gabe said as both brothers looked at the blue luminescent peacock feather tattooed on Gabe's inner wrist.

"No…this…it can't be, what does it mean? "Gabe said.

"I don't know but that's not good this ancient order…" Houston said.

"Bro that's crazy talk, I don't believe it, look when the tattoo radiates blue light, there's something else that shows, a message…"

Both brothers leaned toward Gabe's arm and read the word inscribed within the eye of the feather, they read out loud 'Amicus Sponsi' the tattoo emitted an explosion of light with such force that suddenly the brothers were propelled and fell in opposite directions from each other crashing across the furniture.

"Ugh…my head, what just happened, did you see that?"

"Yeah, more like I lived that and have the bruise to prove it" Houston said holding his elbow, someone knocked on the door.

"I'll get it" Houston said.

"No let me, just so it doesn't look weird, since it's my room" Gabe said.

"It was someone from room service, just wondering about the noise."

"Ok we do really need to look into this further" Houston said.

"Yeah, we do, now I understand."

"Understand what?" Houston said as he began to dress the small wound on his elbow.

"The guy with the tattoo said they were expecting me, they made it easy for me to get in."

"So, they knew you'd come."

"Yeah, they did…so unpredictable" Gabe said staring at the tattoo on his arm.

"Friend Of The Bridegroom," Houston said.

"Beg a pardon?" Gabe replied.

"The tattoo, the Latin word means Friend Of The Bridegroom."

"What? I'm completely lost;" after a long pause Gabe said.

"I'm leaving the day after tomorrow..."

"I know that look, let me guess...and you want to go back there?" Houston asked.

"Yes, I have no choice."

"Are you out of your mind?! Look at what they did to you, obviously they're not regular humans, with regular abilities, they are something more."

"I have to Houston."

"Listen to me Gabe, very carefully, that tattoo means some type of allegiance, and my little research was just a drop in a bucket to what they really are, and what they are capable of" Gabe was silent, as he looked at his brother.

"Ok fine, this time I'm coming with you."

"No, you can't."

"Look bro, it's either I come with you or I tell mom and dad."

"Wow that's cold bro, and you sound like a six-year-old... fine you come along," Houston nodded glad they agreed.

"Gabe the protocluster, look they're glowing on their own, in your tattoo."

"What does it mean?"

"No idea, but my wildest guess would be that it's some kind of a signal."

"We go back tomorrow then," Gabe said.

"Hmm..." Houston said.

Whoosh!

Both brothers looked at the window, the drapes moved from the violent wind, a tall, dark-toned man was standing there, arms crossed, the ancient order tattoo showing on his upper arm, it wasn't the man Gabe saw before, it was someone else, his dark assessing eyes looking at them in a familiar way.

"Gabe, my name's Seth, you need to come with me," the man said with a strange accent.

Gabe shook his head.

"He's not going anywhere..." Houston said.

Seth's gaze was now fixed on Houston, he smiled suddenly, white teeth showing, which strangely enough was much more intimidating.

"Houston, finally it was about time, welcome."

The brothers looked at each other in confusion.

"You both need to come with me."

Houston felt to tread carefully with this Seth guy as somehow, he had an uneasy feeling that his and his little brother's fates were in Jeopardy, their lives could take a major turn and never be the same.

"You have twenty-four hours to get ready, before I return..."

"Amicus Sponsi" he greeted them, placing his right hand on his chest.

The man floated off the ground, and was out the window in a flash, disappearing into the clouds, emitting the same whoosh! sound.

"What in the world..." Gabe said

"There's much more to this tattoo" Houston said.

Gabe was petrified, eyes wide "Big brother?"

"Hmm?" Houston said as he could barely speak.

"We're in big trouble" Gabe felt an immediate sense of urgency, of the inevitable.

"We need to get out of here...now."

excerpt from

UNUSUAL ENCOUNTERS: VOLUME II

PART II: THE SYNDICATES

Coast of MADAGASCAR, ANTANANARIVO, 12:30 pm
MONRODOVA SEA HARBOR

"It's a much larger area than I thought" Jacob Ngoma said

"Something's off about this place" Deputy Lemashi Solomon said

"What do you mean?" Jacob said as Solomon's eyes were slowly scanning the busy dock full of merchants, dockworkers handling and supervising containers.

Solomon wiped a drop of sweat coming from his hairline down to his forehead as he faced Jacob "Let's test these walkies before we split up"

"Allright, do I take North or South"

"You go North, I'll take South, actually let's do this

instead, we try out these transceivers on the way to our destinations."

"Sounds good" Jacob said as he began walking away at the same time as Lemashi was

Solomon stood by a cargo crane and pulled out the transceiver about to begin transmission, when he heard an unusual static "Jacob calling Solomon" Jacob's voice could be heard clearly from the transceiver. Solomon pressed the button "Go ahead" he said

"Well looks like it works" Jacob said the added

"Now I guess it's time to_"

"Shh shh quiet" Solomon said suddenly as he heard the unusual static again.

"what's wrong?" Jacob said

"Someone is piggybacking our frequency"

"What? but that's not possible...ok, I made it to my extract point" Jacob said

"Good, sit tight and remember, no specifics..." Solomon was speaking when suddenly a loud sound echoed in from the transceiver.

"Jacob! What's that sound?"

"I don't know, I heard it coming from in between these two containers on my right"

"interesting" Solomon said

"You were right" Jacob said

"Right about what?" Solomon asked

"About this zone of the Dock, something's definitely not

adding up," Jacob said

"Are you seeing something on your end?" Solomon replied

"Yes, one second ago both cargos I told you about were sitting on dunnage bags about 4 feet apart" Jacob said

"Ok...what about it?" Solomon said

"Now as we speak, these two containers are merged, as if glued together_"

"Impossible, those cargos are about 6,000 pounds each, who could move it_" Solomon said

"Whoa! What's that?"

"What? what's wrong? Hang on I'm coming to you" Solomon said as he began running toward Jacob's extract point.

"Solomon, we got a runner! He phased through the container wall like some invisible man! I'm going after him!"

"What? Jacob, no wait! I'm closing up on your location_"

Hmph! Suddenly Solomon lost balance and fell lying face down on the ground, he could hear the uneven static of the broken transceiver next to him, then he heard two sets of heavy footsteps coming closer, he couldn't see their faces, but knew, he is not alone...that wasn't a good sign...

MEET THE AUTHOR

AZI SOKI is a Christian novelist, originally from the Democratic Republic of Congo, Kinshasa, and has been a Texas resident for many years. She is looking forward to showing forth God's Intimate Glory and Splendor through Creative Writing.

www.ingramcontent.com/pod-product-compliance
Lightning Source LLC
Chambersburg PA
CBHW081135300726
48982CB00005B/971

* 9 7 8 1 0 8 8 0 1 6 8 8 6 *